IT'S A KID'S LIFE
5

CAMP CHAOS

By Kerry Gibb

First published by Packman Publishing in Great Britain in 2019 .

Printed and bound in Great Britain at Clays Ltd, Elcograf S.p.A.

A CIP catalogue record for this title is available from the British Library.

ISBN 978-0-9934937-4-4

OTHER BOOKS IN THE SERIES

Subscribe now to

Author Kerry Gibb

on YouTube for some

videos from behind the scenes, book

reviews, top 10 count downs,

chances to win some great prizes

and much more!

Also follow Kerry Gibb on Facebook,

Instagram and Twitter!

For Liam, Jamie, Danny and Joe, creators of constant chaos who make my world complete.

This is me, Ben, age ten.

Pocket Rocket, my eight-year-old brother.

Big Spud, my five-year-old brother.

Little Spud, my three-year-old brother.

Dad – real dad to my brothers, and technically step-dad to me, but basically, the best dad I could ask for.

Mum – makes great hot chocolate and marshmallows, but can be embarrassing!

Rob – technically my real dad, but never been too good at the dad stuff.

Cassie – Rob's girlfriend and Jodie's Mum.

Jodie – my baby sister.

CHAPTER 1

I focused on my opponent as I heard shouts from the crowd.

"Go on, Ben!"

"Come on Ben, you can do this!"

"Get him Ben!"

I recognised the last squeaky voice as coming from my youngest brother, Little Spud. I glanced over at him to see his excited face smiling as he threw his skinny arms around in what I can only imagine resembled punches. I really needed to give him some training on those. It looked more like he was doing some sort of bizarre dance move!

Focus Ben, I reprimanded myself as I drew my attention back to the task in hand. I was at a karate tournament, my first one since becoming a black belt. Reaching down with my fingertips, I proudly touched the long strip of material tied around my waist. The belt belonging to my Sensei was tatty and faded with age. Mine, on the other hand, was as black as the night's sky and still firm to the touch. It was my most prized possession.

Locking eyes with my opponent, I raised my guard, ready to fight. I was a brave warrior going into battle... I was a daring trooper ready for war... I was a fierce tiger ready to strike...

"Poppet, be careful, he's a bit bigger than you!"

Poppet? POPPET? Had she really just called me "poppet"?

Dropping my guard, I gazed over at my mum in disbelief. How could she be so embarrassing?

"One point," shouted the referee, interrupting the look of horror I was casting in my mum's direction.

Great! Not only had she just called me poppet in front of a room full of people (who were now sniggering at me), but while I'd been distracted, my opponent had taken advantage. He'd directed a sneaky punch at my head, just as the referee had signalled the fight was to start.

Luckily for me, the black belt I was facing had the perfect control you would expect of someone of his level. It was a sign of true skill. He'd been able to launch a fast punch with his fist and then stop with ease so that it only made light contact with me.

Karate tournaments at my age were semi-contact which suited me just fine. I wanted my brain intact thank you very much. I wouldn't be much good at running my own business when I was older if I ended up missing some very valuable brain cells! Karate was all about skill, and it was time for me to forget about my humiliation, courtesy of my own mother, and show everyone what I was made of.

I adjusted my body into a fighting stance.

Blocking out everything else in the room, I fixed my eyes on my opponent. Mum was right. He was slightly bigger than me, but not by much. I waited for him to make another move, biding my time until he left himself open. It was a tactic I had learnt from my Sensei. Sure enough, his impatience got the better of him, and he launched forward with a punch to the head. Expertly, I dodged it and retaliated with my own punch to his chest. Skilfully holding my power as my fist lightly connected with his chest, the referee held up his flag to signal a point for me. Feeling confident, I decided that it was time to try the leg sweep I had been practising all week. Before he knew what was happening, I hooked my leg around the back of my opponent's leg and watched him collapse to the ground.

I took the opportunity to look over at my family who had all come to support me. Mum gave me a big thumbs-up with a cheesy grin on her face.

Pocket Rocket, my eight-year-old brother, was dangling from Dad's arm trying to imitate the leg sweep he had just seen. Needless to say, his skinny leg didn't stand a chance of getting Dad to collapse to the ground. Big Spud, my five-year-old brother, and Little Spud, my three-year-old brother, were doing karate chops on each other's heads, screaming 'hi-yah' as they delivered their pathetic looking blows. Little Spud saw me looking and started waving excitedly. His face suddenly changed to one of anger though as I felt my legs slipping from under me.

I had made the ultimate mistake all over again and let myself get distracted. I had thought my leg sweep would keep my opponent down for at least five seconds, but apparently he wasn't the pushover he had seemed. Seeing his chance, he had sprung back up onto his feet like a cat with nine lives and retaliated with a cheeky copy of the move I had just performed on him.

I fell on my backside with a thud, but not before catching a glimpse of Little Spud running towards us. My opponent was just about to deliver a match-winning strike to my chest when Little Spud launched himself at his legs.

It was only this morning that Pocket Rocket had been teaching him to rugby tackle in the lounge. Little Spud had been instructed to stand in front of the sofa as Pocket Rocket had run at him. He had then grabbed Little Spud round the legs whilst barging his shoulder into his slender frame. Little Spud had found it hilarious as he had tumbled back onto the sofa time and time again. He had obviously picked up a few tips from Pocket Rocket though as, unbelievably, his tiny body managed to knock my opponent right off his feet.

"Get off my brother you nincompoop!" his shrill little voice shouted.

He then sat right on my poor opponent's legs in an attempt to pin him down. I lay there, stunned at what I was seeing. Then, just as I thought it couldn't get any worse, Big Spud ran over and launched himself into the air like he was belly flopping into a swimming pool.

He landed slap bang on the poor boy's tummy. My opponent groaned as he lay there, winded and in shock as to what had just happened.

Coming to my senses, I stood up and picked my brothers up off of him, one by one. The referee glared at them as Mum and Dad ran over to scoop them up, muttering their apologies. Everyone else in the crowd was laughing uncontrollably. I, on the other hand, was absolutely mortified. Next week couldn't come quickly enough. A whole five days away from my annoying little brothers as I got to go on the much-anticipated Year Six residential trip. I could not wait!

CHAPTER 2

"Why did you leave it to the last minute to
pack, Ben?" moaned Mum.

We were in my bedroom the evening after
my karate tournament. I had finally seen
the funny side of my little brother's 'pitch
invasion' onto the karate mat. Luckily, my
opponent had had a good sense of humour
and taken his unexpected rugby tackle
incredibly well. The referee had allowed the
fight to continue, and the winning point
had gone in my favour when I
demonstrated a skilfully timed spinning
kick which lightly brushed my opponent's
cheek, scoring me two points.

"I had other things on my mind," I said,
referring to my karate tournament.

"OK, well I think we are just about
there," Mum said as she pulled the zip of
my suitcase shut.

"I can't believe you're not going to be
here for five whole days!" exclaimed Mum,
looking sad. She enveloped me in a big bear
hug and planted a kiss on my cheek which
I quickly brushed off.

"Yep, five whole days of no annoying little brothers and no annoying parents!" I replied playfully. Mum knew that I was going to miss her really, not that I'd admit that to anyone. Well, maybe to my best friend, Tommy, but definitely nobody else.

"Well I'm going to miss you, and so are your little brothers," said Mum.

"Don't forget Obi and Lola," I said reaching down to tickle our dog, Obi's, soft, furry belly.

"Don't worry, we'll look after them. Pocket Rocket has already said he'll sneak Obi onto his bed with Lola every night."

Typical Pocket Rocket! As if one dog wasn't enough to have sleeping on his bed with him, he was going to take advantage of my absence and have two! At least I knew Obi would be OK with his best pal Lola.

"Right, let's go and have some hot chocolate before bed," said Mum.

Now she was talking. "Can I have extra marshmallows?" I asked, knowing that she would struggle to resist my request as I pulled on her emotional heartstrings. "I won't be able to have any for five days!"

"Well, maybe just this once," said Mum.

"But don't tell your brothers!"

My three younger brothers were already sitting at the table sipping their hot chocolates when we got downstairs.

"Are you going to come back, Ben," asked Little Spud, looking worried. "Pocket Rocket told me you weren't ever coming home again!"

Pocket Rocket did a little snigger through his nose, looking guilty. "You're so gullible!" he exclaimed.

I picked Little Spud up and put him on my lap. He had a hot chocolate moustache above his top lip where he'd been enjoying his bedtime treat.

"Of course I'm coming back," I told my youngest brother as I gave him a gentle tickle in his ribs. "You can't get rid of me that easily."

Little Spud smiled and gave me a big hug. I guess he could be cute when he wanted to be.

Big Spud looked disgruntled. "Does that mean I don't get your bedroom then?" he asked. "Pocket Rocket said I could have it."

I glared at Pocket Rocket. "No, Big Spud, you cannot have my bedroom. I'm going for five days, and when I come back on Friday I expect to find my bedroom exactly how I left it. OK?"

"OK," he said begrudgingly.

"I'm going to set my intruder alarm on my door, so if any of you so much as touch the handle, I'll know about it!" I warned them all.

"How will you know?" asked Pocket Rocket, smugly. "You won't be here."

"Because it will send a message to my phone telling me," I lied. "And if that happens, I've set up stink bombs in each of your bedrooms that I can make explode at the touch of a button."

Big Spud and Little Spud giggled.

"You're lying!" said Pocket Rocket.

"Maybe I am, maybe I'm not," I replied. "But trust me, you don't want to risk it. They smell worse than your feet, mixed with your farts, mixed with your breath when you haven't brushed your teeth," I said, pointing at Pocket Rocket, Big Spud, and Little Spud in turn.

Their little eyes all fixed on me suspiciously. I shrugged my shoulders and scooped a spoonful of marshmallows from my hot chocolate. I knew they didn't totally believe me, but there was enough doubt for them not to risk it.

Pocket Rocket's eyes shifted down to my overflowing mug. "Hey, Mum, why has Ben got more marshmallows than us?"

Mum rolled her eyes at him and swiftly topped up his mug with a small handful of extra marshmallows, and then did the same for my other brothers. They all cheered like they had won the lottery. Mum and I shared a sneaky look, knowing full well that she had only given them a fraction of the amount she had given me. I really should go away and make Mum miss me more often!

CHAPTER 3

I awoke to the sound of my alarm beeping
in my ear and groaned. I hated Monday
mornings. I reached down to cuddle Obi's
soft fur against my body and was just
about to doze back to sleep when I
remembered...

Today wasn't just a normal boring
Monday morning with a week of school
ahead of me. Today was the day I was
setting off on my Year Six residential trip.
Five whole days of fun! My friends and I
had all been talking about it for months
and now the day had finally arrived. I
jumped out of bed and quickly had a
shower. I didn't plan on washing all week,
so Mum had made me promise to have one
last scrub this morning before I left. I set a
new house record for the time taken to get
ready as I gobbled down my breakfast and
got myself dressed.

Pocket Rocket and Big Spud were sitting
at the table eating their cereal one tiny
spoonful at a time, like they had all the
time in the world to get ready. I was

starting to see why Mum always ended up shouting at us to hurry up in the mornings.

"I'm just going to wake Little Spud up," announced Mum. "Ben, can you put your suitcase in the hall so we don't forget it?"

I ran up the stairs two at a time. I was so excited thinking about my week away. I tried to pick my suitcase up with one hand, but it was too heavy so I dragged it along the floor instead. Big Spud appeared at my door.

"Can I sit on your suitcase as you push it down the stairs?" he asked.

We used to take it in turns to sit in the washing basket and whizz down the stairs into the crash barrier at the end, made up of duvets and bean bags. It was so much fun... until one day when I had pushed Pocket Rocket a little bit too hard. He had ended up catapulting out of the basket half way down and flying head first over the top of the crash barrier into the wall. Let's just say that the end-result was a big

lumpy head, a big grumpy Mum, and the end of our days playing washing basket stair whizz!

"OK, but quick before Mum sees us," I said, positioning the suitcase at the top of the stairs. It was so heavy! It must have been the extra jumpers Mum had made me pack. Big Spud climbed on top of the case looking excited.

"Wait one second," I said, as I ran back to grab the duvet, pillows and bean bag from my bedroom. As tempting as it was to send my little brother flying down the stairs with no crash barrier, I wasn't that crazy. Mum would go mad if he got hurt and maybe even ban me from the school trip. Oh, and of course, there was the issue that it was actually quite dangerous and held the real risk of a hospital visit if it went wrong.

"Right, are you ready?" I asked

"Yep!" came his reply as his eyes opened wide with excitement.

"Actually, wait just two more seconds," I said, running back to my bedroom again.

I came back with my skateboarding helmet which I plonked on top of my little

brother's head. He looked a bit worried at
that point.

"Don't worry," I said. "It's just a
precaution."

"This case feels bumpy," he said
wriggling. "There's something sticking up."

"That'll just be my wellies," I said.
"Quick, Mum's coming."

"Can you see if Little Spud is downstairs
please, Ben?" Mum called. "I thought he
was still asleep but he's not in bed."

"Yeah, I'll look," I replied, anxious to
keep her away from the stairs.

"Three, two, one, go!" I whispered to Big
Spud as I gave the case an almighty shove
to send it on its thrill ride down the stairs.

Big Spud let out an excited squeal as he picked up speed. His wasn't the only squeal I heard though!

As the suitcase crashed into the barrier at the bottom of the stairs, Big Spud toppled off giggling.

"That was amazing!" he exclaimed. "Again, again, again!"

But I was more bothered as to where the squeal had actually come from. I raced down the stairs after him and grabbed the case. No wonder it had been so heavy! I tugged at the zip, knowing what I would find inside. I flipped the lid up and there, gazing out at me, looking slightly dizzy and shaken, was Little Spud!

"Hi Ben," he said giggling.

I picked him up out of the suitcase before Mum saw.

"What were you doing in my suitcase?" I demanded. "And where have all my clothes gone?"

"I wanted to come with you," he answered innocently. "I'm going to miss you to the moose and back."

"To the moon and back," I corrected him. "I'm going to miss you to the moon and back, is what you say, not to the moose and back."

"Well that then," he said. "I couldn't fit in with the clothes in so I took them out. Quick, put me back in the cage before Mum sees, so I can come with you."

"It's a case, Little Spud, not a cage. A SUITCASE! And no, I am not putting you back in, because you are NOT coming!"

"Ben, have you found Little Spud," Mum shouted from the bathroom, sounding worried.

"Yep, he's here, Mum," I replied. "He's just having breakfast." I grabbed the now empty suitcase in one hand and Little Spud in the other and raced to the kitchen.

Plonking him down in his chair, I poured some cereal in a bowl, added a splash of milk and gave him a spoon.

"S'not fair," moaned Little Spud, crossing his arms in a huff as he realised that his plan hadn't worked. "Pocket Rocket hid in the car when you went camping with Rob, and he was allowed to stay!"

He was, of course, referring to the time I had gone camping with my real dad, Rob, last year. Rob hadn't been a particularly good dad when I was younger, but since he had had a baby with his new girlfriend, Cassie, he had definitely improved in the dad department. He would never be as good as Dad – technically real dad to all my brothers and step-dad to me – but at least it was a start. Anyway, when he had taken me camping, unbeknown to all of us, Pocket Rocket had hidden on the back seat of the car under some coats. By the time we found him it was too late to take him home and so he had ended up staying with us. Apparently, Little Spud was learning from the master.

"Nice try, Little Spud, but it's not going to happen. Now where are the clothes you emptied out?" I was trying to stay calm so that Mum didn't find out that I had sent not just one, but two little brothers flying down the stairs at top speed.

"Not telling you!" said Little Spud, sulking that he wasn't getting his own way.

I rushed off with my suitcase, knowing that it would be quicker to find the clothes myself. I grabbed the duvet and pillows on my way and shoved them messily back on my bed.

I heard footsteps on the stairs and Mum muttering something about a bean bag. Oops, I had forgotten to grab the bean bag with the pillows and duvet!

Little Spud had dumped all of my clothes in my wash bin. Luckily it had been empty before so I literally tipped it upside down over the suitcase and let everything just tumble back in. I didn't have time to check it was all there so just trusted it was and zipped the case back up. It was much lighter now than the last time I had tried to move it. I picked it up and walked down the stairs.

"Shoes on boys," I heard Mum shout. "It's time to go."

This was one morning I didn't need asking twice. I pulled my trainers on in record time, relishing the fact that I wasn't having to wear school uniform today, and carried my suitcase out to the car.

CHAPTER 4

"EVERYONE STOP TALKING!"
boomed a voice, growing in volume with
each syllable.

The whole class stopped the noise at
once and turned to look at our teacher. Mrs
Jackson was standing at the front of the
classroom with a face as red as a tomato.

"Thank you," she said. "Now, perhaps
you can listen the first time I speak in
future, rather than waiting until I'm
shouting like your mums do when they
have to ask you to get off of your
Playstation for the one hundredth time."

"Um, Mrs Jackson," said Leroy, putting
up his hand.

"Yes, Leroy."

"I don't have a Playstation. I've got an
Xbox."

"Thank you for sharing that with us,"
said Mrs Jackson, sarcastically. "I don't
care if you have a Playstation, an Xbox, or
your dad's old Amstrad from the 1980's.
The point is, I don't intend to raise my voice

at you for the next five days. Understood?"

Leroy nodded his head, not daring to say another word.

"Mrs Jackson's a bit fired up today," I whispered to my best friend, Tommy, who was sitting next to me.

"I heard she hates the school residential as it means that she misses watching all of her favourite reality TV shows," he whispered back.

"I heard that it's because she misses her cat," piped up Nosy Natalie from behind us.

"Anyone who needs the toilet before we leave had better go now as we won't be stopping once we get on the coach. I repeat, we will NOT be stopping," barked Mrs Jackson.

Everyone got up and rushed to the toilets that were outside the classroom door. No one liked the thought of being the one to sit there squirming, with their legs crossed, whilst the rest of the kids teased them by making waterfall noises in their ear.

After what seemed like an eternity, we were finally all seated on the coach ready to go. Just as it was pulling out, a worried voice shouted from the back.

"Wait!"

We all jerked forwards as the driver hit the brakes. It was Tamsin.

"What on earth is the matter?" asked Mrs Jackson, looking back in alarm.

"I've forgotten my passport!" she wailed, looking as though she was about to cry.

Mrs Jackson reached up her left hand and rubbed her eyebrow in exasperation.

"Tamsin, you don't need your passport," she replied calmly. "We're going to the Isle of Wight."

"Is that in Europe, Mrs Jackson," asked Zayan.

"It's part of Great Britain!" exclaimed Mrs Jackson. "I think we should maybe cancel this trip and stay at school for a Geography lesson instead. Honestly children!"

A collective shout of "No," resonated around the coach as we imagined a week of school instead of a week at an amazing residential activity centre.

Much to our relief, we felt the coach pull

away again. This was it. The week we had all been looking forward to for so long was finally here. It was going to be the best week of my life!

"Did you bring any sweets?" I asked Tommy, nudging him with my elbow. He had managed to bagsy the window seat in a game of rock, paper, scissors that we held last week. I always beat my younger brothers with a well-timed wrap of paper around their rock, but I had met my match with Tommy.

"Yep, I have a whole stash in a secret compartment in my suitcase," he replied with a wink.

"What about for now though?" I asked. "We need some for the journey." I pulled a large bag of pear drops out of my coat pocket and offered one to Tommy.

He shook his head as he took one. "I didn't think of that," he said.

"Don't worry, we can share these," I said, positioning the bag of sweets between us on the seat.

"Did someone say sweets?" came a voice from the seat behind.

I pushed myself up and around awkwardly to see who it was. My friend Josh smiled back at me and reached out his hand.

"OK, but just one," I said. "And don't tell anybody."

I plonked a yellow pear drop (my least favourite) in his hand and went to turn back around in my seat.

"Uh-hum" said another voice, stopping me in my tracks. Samuel, who had been staring out of the window next to Josh had suddenly snapped out of his daydream and wanted a sweet too!

I rolled my eyes and plopped a pear drop in his outstretched hand – another yellow one of course. I couldn't have them all eating my favourite red ones. They were sacred!

The next hour passed quickly thanks to Tommy and I playing a game of 'Would you rather?'

"OK, my turn," I said.

"Would you rather eat a whole raw onion or a suck a lemon for ten seconds?"

"Definitely suck a lemon!" Tommy replied confidently. "Pocket Rocket dared me to suck a lemon last time I was round at your house and it actually wasn't too bad once I got past the horrible feeling you get in your jaw."

I pulled a *sucked lemon face* myself just at the thought of it. Urgh!

"Would you rather eat broccoli flavoured ice cream or strawberry flavoured slugs?" Tommy threw back at me.

I thought for a second before shrugging my shoulders and saying, "I'm going to have to go with strawberry flavoured slugs. My mum once made me drink one of those disgusting juices she makes and it had broccoli in it. I literally threw up all over the kitchen floor. It was revolting! So broccoli flavoured ice cream is definitely a no-no for me."

"OK, well strawberry flavoured slugs it is then," said Tommy laughing.

"I've got one," said Zayan, leaning across the aisle of the coach. "Would you rather hold one poisonous snake or sit in a bath of fifty non-poisonous snakes?"

"Sit in the bath!" Tommy and I replied in unison.

"Yep, me too," agreed Zayan. "One bite from the poisonous snake and you'd be a gonna!"

"Can I play?" asked Jessica, poking her nose in between the seats in front of us. She was sitting next to her friend Maisie who was busy pressing the anti-sickness bands on her wrists, looking worried.

"Maisie feels sick, and I'm getting bored."

"OK, I said. "But make it good. None of this 'would you rather be a unicorn or a fairy' rubbish!"

"Fine," said Jessica in an exasperated voice as she rolled her eyes at me. She thought for a second and then said, "Would you rather kiss Emily or Mrs Jackson?"

I sat there unable to answer. Of course I couldn't say that I'd kiss a teacher, but I also couldn't say that I'd kiss Emily, aka Evil Emily! We had history! She'd become my arch-enemy a while ago. I couldn't say her. Tommy and Zayan both replied "Emily" as I sat there looking for an escape route.

"Come on Ben," pushed Jessica. "Mrs Jackson or Emily?"

Barely opening my mouth, I muttered "Emily" through clenched teeth.

"Pardon," said Jessica, loving seeing me squirm.

"Emily," I said a little louder.

"There you go," said Jessica. "That wasn't so hard now, was it?"

Before I could respond that actually, that was harder than she could possibly imagine, Mrs Jackson loudly informed us that we had arrived at the ferry port.

"Last one," said Tommy quickly. "Would you rather do a loud fart on a crowded coach or a silent smelly fart!"

Jessica, Zayan and I were just about to answer when Tommy started giggling and the pungent smell hit our nostrils.

"Ew, Tommy!" Jessica exclaimed, covering her nose with her hand. "That's gross!"

Thank goodness it was time to escape the stuffy coach and get some fresh air on the ferry. Top deck here I come!

CHAPTER 5

"Now, it's very important that we all stay inside," said Mrs Jackson "I don't want to have to call anyone's parents to tell them that we've lost one of you overboard. Understood?"

What? No top deck? That was the best part of going on a ferry. Inside smelt of badly fried food mixed with fumes from the engines.

We had all just clambered off the coach and climbed the staircase to the middle deck. The noise of the engines was intense until we popped through the heavy door held ajar by Mr Wallis, the teacher of the other Year Six class. I had been looking forward to the fresh air on the top deck, but Mrs Jackson had just squashed that hope entirely.

"This will be our main seating area," continued Mrs Jackson. She swept her hand in the air indicating a few rows of tatty looking seats. They looked like they had been there for the past forty years, maybe only getting cleaned once a month if they were lucky. I shuddered as I imagined all of the bottoms that had sat on them before mine.

"But you are welcome to wander around this deck," Mrs Jackson said. "There's a cinema at the end of this corridor and a little shop where you can buy snacks or souvenirs at the other end. Do not, I repeat DO NOT, go into the arcade next to the shop. Do not go anywhere on your own. And do not leave this deck."

There were an awful lot of *do nots* in that sentence. Mrs Jackson really should look into getting a thesaurus to expand her vocabulary. I chuckled to myself as I thought of this. For the past few months she had been ramming grammar and punctuation down our throats in preparation for our end of primary school tests. She obviously needed to take some of her own advice! The exams had taken place two weeks ago and now we were free. I never wanted to see another practice test paper for as long as I lived.

"Come on, Ben," said Tommy. "Let's go and see which movies are showing."

"You won't get to watch a movie," smirked Nosey Natalie. "The ferry only takes forty-five minutes.

"Alright Little Miss Know-It-All," I said as I pulled a face at her. I know it was a bit childish and the sort of thing my little brothers would do, but I couldn't help myself - I just found her so annoying!

"I knew that," Tommy said quickly as his cheeks flushed red. "I thought they might have a cartoon or something."

We marched off past Nosey Natalie as she stood there, smirking with her group of equally annoying friends. Tommy looked at me.

"She is right though," he said. "They definitely won't be showing a movie. What shall we do instead?"

"There's always the arcade," I said, raising my left eyebrow at my friend.

"You heard what Mrs Jackson said though," Tommy replied. "We're not allowed to go into the arcade. We don't want to get in trouble before we've even arrived on the Isle of Wight."

"Then let's make sure we don't get caught," I replied in the casual way that I knew always worked with Tommy. If I acted like it was no big deal, he would relax more and just go with it.

"But what about these hi-vis jackets they've made us put on," he pointed out, tugging at the edge of the fluorescent yellow material. "We'll stick out like a sore thumb in them."

"Easy," I said checking over my shoulder to make sure no one was watching. "We just take them off and hide them up our jumpers." I slipped my jacket off quick as a flash and scrunched it up underneath my over-sized hoodie. "Come on, let's go before the others catch us up!"

Tommy reluctantly whipped his jacket off and stuffed it up his own jumper before following me down the corridor in the direction of the arcade.

I wobbled as the ferry swayed from side to side over the choppy waves. "I hope no one gets sea-sick," I said to Tommy over my shoulder. He didn't reply. Was it me or was his skin starting to look a shade of green?

We reached the entrance to the arcade in about ten seconds flat. You couldn't miss it with its flashing lights shining out into the otherwise drab décor.

Excitedly, I walked into the entrance, but my face quickly fell. "Is this it?" I asked no one in particular.

The arcade consisted of just three slot machines, each of them labelled *Over 18's only* and one laser game which looked like it had been borrowed from the 1990's.

"Let's just go," said Tommy.

"We may as well have a quick go now we're here," I said as I fished into my trouser pocket trying to find a 50p coin.

"Ben, I don't feel so well," said Tommy.

"It's just a bit of sea sickness I told my friend as I focused on where I needed to put my coin into the slot. "Here, it's a two player game. You take this laser and shoot at all the weird alien looking things that flash up on the screen."

I thrust the laser at him and grabbed my own one. The machine jumped to life as it started flashing and making scary alien noises. I aimed and pulled the trigger. Years of going to the arcade with my real dad, Rob, had made me a pro at games like this, even if this one was nearly as old as Rob himself. I had a flashback of an image of Pocket Rocket and me playing in the arcade at a campsite whilst Rob had been drinking at the bar. Looking back, it had been really great to have my little brother there. He did make a good wingman. This time Tommy would be my wingman.

But suddenly, Tommy was making a weird noise and before I could turn my head to see what the problem was, the screen in front of us had been splattered with a yellowy green gunge. It dripped down to the floor in long clumps of sticky mucus and the smell hit my nostrils before I even had a chance to block my nose. It was pungent with a hint of fruitiness.

Pear drops I thought to myself!

"I told you I didn't feel well," muttered Tommy as he dropped his laser and wrapped his arms around his tummy. "I think I might have eaten too many pear drops on the coach."

"I think you're right," I said as I dropped my own laser and stared at my friend.

"I think I'd better go and sit down," said Tommy.

We snuck out of the arcade together as quickly as we'd snuck in. I felt sorry for the poor person who would have to come and clean the arcade after this crossing. Although, judging by the cleanliness of the rest of the ferry, Tommy's sick would still be smeared down the arcade machine five years from now! I screwed my face up at the thought. Gross!

I led Tommy back to our designated seating area where we found Mrs Jackson. There were a few other children sitting with her looking a similar shade of green to Tommy.

"Mrs Jackson, Tommy isn't feeling too good," I told her.

"Oh dear Tommy, come and sit here with

me. I'll give you a little sick bag just in case. Where are your high vis jackets you two?"

Oops, we had forgotten to put them back on after hiding them up our jumpers. "We were worried about getting sick on them," I said, thinking on my feet.

"Maybe I should take a couple of these guys out on deck," Mr Wallis said, "they could do with a bit of fresh air."

"Oh no, we can't possibly do that," replied Mrs Jackson frowning. "They could all fall in and drown. What would I tell their parents?"

Well, that's a bit dramatic, I thought. But at least Mr Wallis had distracted her from the high-vis interrogation.

"I promise I'll look after them," Mr Wallis replied calmly. "I suffered sea sickness myself as a child so know how it feels. These poor kids need some air. I'm starting to feel a little queasy myself if I'm being honest. I'll keep them far back from the railings, I promise."

Tommy retched into the paper bag Mrs Jackson had given him.

"Well maybe just a few minutes wouldn't

hurt," she said reluctantly. "But only the children who are sea-sick. No one else!"

Tommy and three other children stood up from their seats and started to follow Mr Wallis towards the exit.

"Shall we play a nice game of *Eye Spy*, Ben?" Mrs Jackson asked me.

Hmmm, Eye Spy or escaping to top deck, I asked myself. It was no contest. It was time to summon up my best acting skills.

"OK," I replied in my sweetest voice possible. "I spy with my little eye, something beginning with s...s...s." I made a grab for the bundle of sickness bags that Mrs Jackson had left on the table. Copying Tommy's retching action, I mimicked him to perfection.

"Sorry," I said wiping my brow. "I think I need some fresh air, too. Not waiting for a reply, I ran off after Mr Wallis and slotted in place next to Tommy. No way was I missing out on a trip out to the top deck!

CHAPTER 6

"And that, kids, is the Isle of Wight," said Mr Wallis, pointing out to sea. Sure enough, land was clearly visible up ahead. It had been a quick crossing.

"Better tell Tamsin to get her passport ready," I said jokingly.

"Nice to see you're feeling better Ben," said Mr Wallis, raising his eyebrows. Something told me that he didn't quite believe my little bout of sea sickness had been genuine, but he didn't seem too bothered.

It was just Maisie, Tommy and I outside with Mr Wallis now as the others had eagerly gone back inside as soon as they had felt better. Mrs Jackson had scared them all into thinking they would fall overboard at the slightest jerk of the boat as we bumped over the waves.

"Did you know the length of the Isle of Wight's only twenty-three miles from one end to the other," I asked Mr Wallis.

"No Ben, I didn't," he replied.

"Which end though?" asked Maisie.

"I don't know, the biggest end, I guess," I told her.

"Yes, but east to west or north to south?" said Tommy.

"The biggest end," I repeated, not liking my knowledge being questioned. It was like having little brothers here with me asking *why, why, why!*

"East to west," responded Mr Wallis. "That's the biggest stretch of land."

"Ok, east to west then," I agreed.

"That's really interesting Ben," applauded Mr Wallis. "Very good general knowledge."

"Did you know a snail can sleep for three years?" said Maisie, wanting to show off her good general knowledge too.

"Um, no, I didn't know that," replied Mr Wallis. "Very good general knowledge to you too, Maisie."

Maisie smiled, looking pleased with herself, before randomly blurting out "Did you know you can hypnotise a frog by putting it on its back and gently stroking its tummy?"

"No, I can't say I knew that either, Maisie," said Mr Wallis. "Again, very interesting, thank you. Who wants to hear an interesting fact about the sea?"

We all nodded.

"Did you know that icebergs can supply water to cities full of people, and that there's a company somewhere that's planning to tow an iceberg from Antarctica to the coast of a really hot country where they get hardly any rain, so that it can provide millions of people with water? How amazing is that?"

"That is amazing," I exclaimed.

"Did you know it's not just a tiger's skin that's striped?" said Tommy, wanting to join in the '*did you know*' competition. "If you shave their fur off, you'll see that their skin is striped too."

"Wow, I did not know that," I said, genuinely impressed with this bit of trivia.

"Did you know that sea otters hold hands whilst they sleep?" said Maisie. "Isn't that cute?"

"We saw that video at school too, Maisie," I said. It's not because they're cute and soppy, it's so they don't float away from each other!"

Maisie huffed and crossed her arms, clearly not impressed with my input.

"Did you know birds can sleep with one eye shut and one eye open so they can keep an eye out for predators coming to eat them?" I said.

"Did you know that my mum's hair is actually naturally grey and not blond like she tells everyone?" said Maisie not wanting to be outdone by me and Tommy.

"OK, you win," said Mr Wallis, holding up his hands. "There's no way any of us can beat that one." He gave Tommy and I a wink as Maisie sat there looking smug. "Plus we have run out of time as, although this chat has been fun, we have to go below deck to get back on the coach. We're just about to dock."

We had been so engrossed in our bizarre *'did you know'* competition chat that we hadn't even noticed how near we had been getting to land. We were now so close that you could almost touch it. I felt a bubble of excitement rising up inside of me. Just a short trip on the coach and we'd be there!

CHAPTER 7

Squashed back on the coach, you could hear a hum of excited chatter amongst everyone. We had been looking forward to this trip all year. Year Six camps were legendary! There wasn't a child in the school who hadn't heard the stories passed down from kids who had been here before us. The water sports were the activities I was most looking forward to. Apparently, last year, one of the kids had to be rescued out at sea when their dingy went out of control, and they had started sailing towards France!

"Help! Je suis out of control!"

And, of course, there were the tales of midnight feasts and pranks on the teachers.

"I think this is it!" exclaimed Tommy, peering out of the window. I leant over him to get a better look. We had just pulled off the main road and were now on a long driveway with sea views. I could just about make out the white tips of the breaking waves as they crashed to shore.

The coach pulled up next to a big sign saying *Welcome to Komodo Camp*.

A big cheer resonated around the coach as Mrs Jackson stood up and announced that we had arrived.

"OK children. Now I know that you're all keen to see where you'll be sleeping so as soon as you've climbed off the coach, we can take our luggage to the dormitories. Girls – you will come with me, and boys – you go with Mr Harris."

There were six teachers with us altogether. Mrs Jackson and Mr Harris were the ones in charge but there were also two teaching assistants, a Year Five teacher, and Mr Skills, the sports teacher who worked part-time.

"I hope we're in the same dorm," I said to Tommy.

Last week, we'd all had to write down the names of three people we'd like to share a room with but would only find out who we were with when we got here.

"We'll be together, I'm sure of it!" said Tommy confidently.

I got out of my seat and climbed off the coach. The warm sunshine hit my face immediately. It seemed as though I'd be needing that sun cream Mum had made me pack. I grabbed my suitcase from the pile that the driver was making as he hauled the cases from the luggage compartment. It wasn't nearly so heavy now that it actually had my clothes in it rather than Little Spud!

"Right, follow us then, boys," said Mr Harris, leading the way to the building up ahead. We walked towards a single storey building that looked like a giant bungalow. It was a murky grey colour and looked very uninviting. Inside was a communal lounge area with a hallway leading from it. Mr Harris stopped us all in the lounge and started to read the much-anticipated list of roommates.

I waited anxiously to hear my name called alongside Tommy's. Every other boy in the room seemed to be called first. It was so frustrating. Finally, Mr Harris said, "and last but not least, we have a group who will be sleeping in the new safari tent just behind this building. Charlie, Noah, Ryan, Jayden, Tommy, and Ben."

"Yes!" Tommy and I exclaimed in unison, giving each other a little fist bump. Not only had we been put together, but we had totally lucked out and been put in the safari tent. Last time I went camping I had been traumatised forever by the creepy crawlies. A safari tent was different, though. I had seen this on the website when Mum had looked up Komodo Camp to see where I was going. It was a brand new tent with a proper wood floor in it and real bunk beds with mattresses and everything.

"That's not fair," piped up Zayan. "Why do they get to go in the safari tent?"

"Because," said Mr Wallis, "the room they were supposed to be in had a group of teenagers last week who thought it would be funny to hide a tuna sandwich in there. The staff only found it this morning, tucked into a crack in the wall. Unfortunately, the smell has lingered and they thought it would be unfair to make anyone sleep in there until it had cleared."

Much respect to those teenagers, I thought. Thanks to them, Tommy and I had now got the best accommodation... brand new... stylish... and further away from the teachers than the rest of them. Perfect!

"You've got half an hour to unpack your things and settle in to your rooms. Then we meet back here for lunch followed by our first activity of the week," announced Mr Wallis.

"I bagsy top bunk," I shouted to Tommy as the six of us who had lucked out ran towards the door. This trip was getting better by the second.

CHAPTER 8

The six of us ran to the safari tent like our lives depended on it. I was just about to make it to the entrance first when Charlie shot ahead of me. He was nearly as fast as Pocket Rocket!

"Wow," I heard him say, just before I ran inside behind him. We were quickly joined by the other boys we were sharing with. All of us paused for a second to take in our surroundings and then, as if coming to our senses all at once, we darted towards the bunk beds. Everyone wanted top bunk status!

I charged at the one furthest away, thinking tactically that everyone would go for the closest option. I was right! Putting one foot on the ladder, I flung myself over the safety bar and lay on the mattress, stating my claim. Tommy got there a millisecond behind me.

"You wanna swap?" he asked hopefully. "I think the bottom bunk might be a little wider."

"Nice try!" I said to my best friend. "Nope,

I'm perfectly comfortable up here, thank you very much."

"Are you absolutely sure?" he asked, not giving up.

It was time to show Tommy that I wasn't budging. Tensing my stomach, I pushed out a nice loud fart.

"Well OK, if you really want to," I said, grinning at him.

"Urgh, you're gross Ben. No way would I sleep in that bed after you've farted on it!"

"I love it when a plan comes together," I said, laughing.

Tommy climbed on the first step of the ladder and swatted me playfully on the head with his pillow.

"Pillow fight!" yelled Ryan, charging over from the other side of the room. Before I knew it, I had been attacked from all angles by five crazy ten year olds. Actually, make that three crazy ten year olds and two equally crazy eleven year olds. Noah and Jayden had already had their birthdays

whilst the rest of us were still waiting. I had no idea what to do for my eleventh. It would be pretty hard to top the amazing nerf gun party I'd had for my tenth birthday. That was epic!

"OK, OK, I give up," I said, after batting away the twentieth pillow flying towards me. These boys were more relentless than my younger brothers.

"Let's get our stuff unpacked so we can go to lunch. I'm starving."

"Me too," said Tommy. "Everything in my tummy got sicked up on the ferry."

The others all went back to their respective beds. Charlie and Jayden had managed to bagsy the top bunks like me. Noah had bottom bunk underneath Charlie and Ryan was with Jayden. Next to each set of bunk beds there was a tiny chest of drawers.

"You have the top drawer," I said to Tommy. "I'll have the bottom one, seeing as I got top bunk."

Tommy just stared at me. "You're so kind!" he said sarcastically. "Having the top drawer is absolutely one hundred percent as important as getting top bunk."

"There's just no pleasing some," I said, giving Tommy a playful shove as he bent down to open his suitcase.

I opened my own and pulled the pile of clothes out. I had forgotten I'd carelessly dumped them back in there after Little Spud had emptied it. Everything was all crumpled. I tried to fold it all before putting it in the drawer. How did Mum do that so easily when she put my clean washing in a pile at home? I gave up after two badly folded T-shirts and started to roll stuff instead.

"You know that is actually a thing?" said Tommy.

"What's a thing?" I asked.

"Rolling your clothes up. It's meant to save space."

"Well that's good, seeing as this tiny drawer is all I have," I replied.

I bunged the rest of my clothes in the chest. As I picked up my wellies which had been at the bottom of the case, I noticed an envelope stuffed inside them.

Pulling it out, I recognised Mum's neat handwriting. I quickly stuffed it under my pillow before the other boys saw it. How embarrassing! Why did Mum have to do things like that? I was only away for four nights. Did she really need to write me a note saying how much she missed me? At least, I presumed that's what it was. Unless, it was some secret snacks she had snuck in for me! School had very specifically said that no sweets were allowed to be brought along on the trip as apparently they would make us all hyper. Teachers could be so boring sometimes. I reached my hand under my pillow and felt the envelope for bumps. To my disappointment, it was flat as a pancake. Nope, there was nothing in there other than a soppy note from my embarrassing mum! At least I had the secret stash of sweets I had brought with me to sell to the other kids.

Suddenly, I heard Charlie and Noah laughing. Oh no, had they seen the note I had just hidden?

"Ryan's got a blankie!" exclaimed Noah.

"I hope you packed your dummy too!"

said Charlie, laughing.

"Shut up you two!" said Ryan. "It's not mine!"

He quickly stuffed the *blankie* back into his suitcase, his cheeks glowing red.

"It's my little sister's. She must have dropped it in there when I was packing!"

I felt sorry for Ryan. I knew what it was like to have younger siblings who did stuff like that.

"Yeah, shut up you two," I said, defending him. "I bet you both brought a teddy with you. Come on, let's see in your cases."

Noah and Charlie squirmed uncomfortably.

"I only brought one cos he's my lucky mascot," said Noah.

"Yeah, me too!" Charlie quickly agreed, liking the sound of that excuse.

Reaching into the pocket of my suitcase, I pulled out a cuddly toy dog. "And I brought this one because it's got my dog's hair inside it."

"You put your dog inside there?" asked Charlie with a look of horror. He wasn't the brightest of kids!

"No, of course not," I said, rolling my eyes. "Last time he had a haircut, I kept some of it and stuffed it inside this toy dog."

"Well that's a bit weird," said Ryan.

"You're the one who brought your sister's blankie with you," I snapped back. If he was going to tease me then he could forget my solidarity with his blankie mishap.

"Everything OK in here, boys?" asked Mr Skills as he appeared at the door.

"Wow, you boys have done alright, haven't you? This is better than mine and Mr Wallis' room, you jammy lot!"

I'd been so busy making sure that I'd got top bunk and unpacking my stuff that I hadn't really noticed the rest of the tent. I looked around me now. The bunk beds were lined up in a 'C' shape at one end. At the other end, there was a cosy, fluffy rug in the middle of four big wicker chairs, covered in lots of colourful cushions. Behind the bunk beds was a curtain that I hadn't notice before. When pulled over to one side, it revealed a metal bucket.

"Erm, why is there a bucket there, Mr Skills?" asked Tommy.

Mr Skills laughed. "Well, the one downside of having this glamorous safari tent, Tommy, is that you don't have a bathroom. You'll need to pop back to the bathrooms in the main block to shower and use the loo. The bucket's there in case you get caught short in the night."

"You mean wee in the bucket?" Tommy asked wide-eyed. It was a far cry from the luxury en-suite he was used to at home.

"Yep, exactly that," replied Mr Skills. "Now come on you lot, you're late for lunch.

With that we all traipsed out of the tent eager to fill our rumbling tummies with food. Legend had it that the food here was amazing!

CHAPTER 9

We weren't disappointed. The food really was amazing! I chose a bacon and egg butty, dripping with ketchup. It was delicious.

With everyone nicely full from lunch, Mrs Jackson hushed us all so that she could tell us about the afternoon's activities.

"This afternoon, children, you have a choice of activities here at camp. Firstly, I will be running a bird watching session down in the woods which will be very exciting."

Tommy and I looked at each other and rolled our eyes. It was safe to say that neither of us would be choosing to sit still watching birds for hours. Mrs Jackson obviously had a very different interpretation to us of the word *exciting*.

"Secondly," Mrs Jackson continued, "you have the option of going to the pottery studio on site and making your own mug with Mr Wallis."

Well, that sounded slightly better.

"And lastly," said Mrs Jackson, you have

the option to join our designated camp leader, Luke, to get a rush of adrenaline on the giant swing."

Now she was talking! I didn't need to ask Tommy which option he was going to choose. She had us at the words 'rush of adrenaline'!

"Anyone for the swing, come and join me over here," I heard a deep voice boom from behind me.

The voice belonged to a man who looked about thirty. He had floppy brown hair hanging over his forehead, and he was wearing combat trouser with a T-shirt saying Komodo Camp. This must be Luke.

About thirty-five of us rushed over to him at once. Roughly twenty children moved over to Mr Wallis. Only five were left with Mrs Jackson.

"Are you sure no more of you want to join us for a spot of bird watching," asked Mrs Jackson, looking a bit rejected. "I've got some cakes we can eat whilst we're waiting," she added, hopefully.

The mention of cake encouraged six people to leave our group for the bird watching crew. It would take more than a bribe of cake to tempt me away from an afternoon of excitement. It probably wasn't even a chocolate cake, but a boring, stale old walnut cake like your great-grandparents would offer you.

"OK, let's go team," said Luke. He grabbed a pile of harnesses as we followed him out of the building. "We've got about a fifteen-minute walk to the equipment which will be perfect for letting your lunch go down. We wouldn't want any of you bringing it back up as you're swinging high off the ground above the rest of us. Hahahahaha!"

He had a big, booming laugh that seemed to echo around us. A few of the kids started to look a little nervous as they realised what they were about to do.

I wondered if anyone would be like Mum was when we went to Cornwall on holiday one year. Dad had taken us to a place called Adrenaline Quarry where a fifty meter long zip-wire had hung from a tall cliff above a lake. We had all queued up for an hour to take our turn. Even Little Spud and Big Spud had been allowed to do it. They'd been beyond excited at being able to do a big boy activity without being told they were too young. But, when Mum got in the harness she totally freaked out, screaming that she didn't want to do it. It had been so embarrassing!

I was about to tell Tommy this story when I spotted a giant swing up ahead that was literally hanging over the top of a cliff!

"And this, kids, is your first glimpse of what you're about to do," announced Luke.

A group of girls in front of me grabbed each other's hands in terror.

"Is it too late to turn back and do the pottery?" asked a girl called Charlotte who had gone white as a sheet.

"You've got nothing to worry about,"

replied Luke. "We're all here to support you. Right team?" he asked, signalling to the rest of us.

We all nodded and collectively muttered "yes".

"I can't hear you!" shouted Luke. "Are we a team?"

"YES," we all shouted, louder this time.

"Good," said Luke. "This isn't just about getting an adrenaline rush. It's about facing your fears. Growing your confidence. Trusting each other, and working as a team. You don't have to do anything you don't want to do, but trust me, if any of you leave here today without trying this amazing activity, you will most definitely regret it. Now let's get up there!"

What he had told us would be a fifteen minute walk was actually more like half an hour by the time we reached the top of the cliff. It was a hot day and the sun was beating down on our heads. I felt thankful that the teachers had made us all bring our water bottles as I took a big gulp from mine.

"Like I said," said Luke, "we're a team, and we're going to trust each other. Two of you will go in the swing together and two more of you will push the lever to get it going. The further you push it, the further you will swing out over the cliff edge, and the higher you will go. If at any time, you get scared and want to stop, shout to your team mates and they will stop the swing for you. Any questions?"

I put my hand up.

"Yes," said Luke, pointing at me.

"Can I go first?" I asked.

"Yes you can, young man!" Luke replied. "What's your name?"

"Ben," I replied

"Does anyone else want to be brave enough to go first with Ben?"

I nudged Tommy, urging him to put his hand up. He hesitated too long though and a girl in my class called Sophia shot her hand up. "I'll do it," she said.

"Great, come on you two, let's show everyone how it's done," said Luke.

Sophia and I walked over to him and the three of us led the way to the giant swing. I would have preferred it if I was doing it with Tommy, but Sophia was nice enough. Plus, if she had the guts to step up to the mark first with me, then she was alright in my book. Imagine if Evil Emily had been the one to put up her hand. She would probably have pushed me out of the swing as we soared above the cliff top! I shuddered at the thought.

Once we reached the swing, Luke got us to sit in a circle, well away from the edge of the cliff. He told us that as this was a trust building exercise, we were going to choose the people who would operate the lever by pointing to someone in the circle. The only catch was, he would be putting a blindfold on us, and spinning us around in the middle of the circle three times before asking us to choose.

Sophia went first, giggling away as Luke spun her around. Looking wobbly, she thrust her finger out in the direction of her friend Grace. As Luke pulled her blindfold off, Sophia ran over and hugged Grace, knowing that she could trust her.

"OK, now your turn, Ben," said Luke.

I made a mental note of where Evil Emily was sitting so that I could make sure I avoided her at all costs. Surely I could keep track of my direction even if I was blindfolded? Three spins round wasn't many.

Luke spun me round again, again, and again. "And one more for luck," he said, as he spun me round a fourth time.

"Hey, that's four spins," I said, as I lost my balance and toppled slightly to the left. Everyone laughed and I tried to pinpoint Tommy's laugh so that I could pick him to pull the lever. Feeling confident that I had located him, I reached my right hand out and pointed with my index finger.

Luke whipped the blindfold off and I came face to face with my chosen one. Zayan! Thank goodness. It wasn't Tommy, but at least it was someone I liked. Come to think of it, I think I was just relieved it wasn't Evil Emily that I had chosen. I would have picked my headmaster, Mr Growler, over her, and that's saying something given our history!

Sophia and I walked over to where the swing was pulled back safely away from the cliff edge. Luke told us to take off our shoes and sit on the seat. I had a moment of panic when I saw that the metal frame was just a metre or so away from the edge of the cliff.

What if the cliff started to erode and it crumbled away as we were swinging?

I felt my heart pumping hard in my chest. My hands went sweaty and I got a strange sensation in my legs. Maybe it hadn't been such a good idea to go first after all? Had I been showing off? Had I been trying to impress everyone, hoping that it would get back to Lottie, my school friend who now lived in Australia? There had been a time I'd once hoped she might be my girlfriend before she had emigrated with her family. Why couldn't I just be more like Tommy and merge into the pack with everyone?

"OK, just slip your arms into these harnesses here and we'll get you guys swinging," said Luke.

I now understood how Mum had felt when she'd freaked out on that zip wire. I couldn't ask to get down though. I'd be the laughing stock of the entire school. Ten years from now, kids would still be relaying the story of the cocky Year Six kid who'd jumped at the chance of being the first to go on the giant swing and then had lost his bottle like a baby. No, I couldn't let that happen. I had to be brave. I had to man-up.

"Eek, this is so exciting!" Sophia said in a shrill voice next to me.

"I know, so exciting," I lied, in a voice that definitely sounded a few pitches higher than my normal voice.

OK, focus, I told myself. *Put a big fake smile on your face and pretend you're enjoying it. Then just try really hard not to pee your pants.*

Luke started a countdown and everyone joined in.

"Ten, nine, eight..."

My mouth felt as dry as if I had face planted in a pile of sand. Sophia joined in the counting but I couldn't speak.

"Seven... six... five... four... three... two...

one!"

I felt the swing moving forward as everyone shouted 'one'. It crept just to the edge of the cliff and then swung back again. *Oh, that wasn't so bad,* I thought.

This was just the beginning though. The next push took us a little further over the edge and the next push, a little further still.

"Do you want to go higher?" shouted Zayan. Before I could answer, Sophia had shouted "Yesss!"

I glanced at her in disbelief. How could she actually be enjoying this!

"This is amazing!" she said, grinning at me.

"Yeah, amazing!" I lied.

I closed my eyes and hoped it would end quickly. That only made it worse though. The sensation in my tummy heightened as it felt like it was leaving my body with every movement forward.

"Woo-hoo!" Sophia cried.

The swing went so high on the next push that all I could see was the blue sky with little fluffy clouds dotted around it like pieces of cotton wool. And then, suddenly, this image was replace by the dry, dusty ground appearing below me as we whizzed backwards again.

"Any time you want to stop, just say," shouted Luke. "Trust your friends to control the leaver."

I wanted to say STOP! Oh how I wanted to. But I just couldn't. Maybe if I just held out a little longer, I'd start to enjoy it. Like when I'd been half way down the zip wire and realised I wasn't going to fall. I gripped tightly to my harness and gave myself a stern talking to. *No way would the teachers let us do something like this if it wasn't one hundred percent safe. Luke had been on this swing hundreds of times and he was still here to tell the tale. I was going to be fine. I was going to be fine. I was going to be fine.* I was repeating this mantra to myself in my head when Sophia grabbed my hand.

"Let's hold our hands up really high for the last few swings," she said.

I did as I was told and felt the adrenaline suddenly bursting through me.

I was OK. I wasn't falling out. I was flying through the air like a bird. My little pep talk to myself had worked.

"Do you want to go higher?" Grace shouted.

"Yes," we both yelled back in unison as we went flying through the air again. As we hurtled back, Luke shouted, "that's it, guys. Time for someone else to have a go now."

Grace and Zayan stopped pulling the lever and the swing gradually slowed to a stop. Just as I had started to squash my nerves and enjoy myself, the ride had stopped. Typical!

"That was amazing," I said as Luke unstrapped me.

"Awesome," said Luke. "You had me a little worried there when you first got on, but you nailed it. Totally controlled your fear. Much respect to you, little dude."

Oh no, not another grown-up who thought it was cool to say *dude*. When would they learn? And *'little dude'*? Come on! I'd let it slide this time though. I was far too hyped up to let something like that bother me.

"Who's going next?" asked Luke. A mass of hands all shot up at once. I think we had successfully helped everyone get over their fear, even if a tiny bit of wee may have escaped into my pants in the process!

CHAPTER 10

The next hour was so much fun. Everyone climbed onto the swing looking like they had been asked to jump into a live volcano, and came off it looking like they had had the best experience of their lives. It was exhilarating.

The last pair to take their turn on the swing was a boy called Elliot from the other class and none other than Evil Emily. They stood in the centre of the circle blindfolded and took it in turns to be spun around before choosing their 'trust buddy' as we had all started referring to the role. Elliot went first and pointed in the direction of a girl called Becky. Emily went next. Luke spun her round three times and then stopped her right opposite me. I stood silently, not wanting her to know where I was. I was sure she would move again slightly. Hardly anyone had literally pointed straight ahead of them. But, as if in slow motion, Emily did just that. Lifting her arm slowly and deliberately, enjoying the attention on her no doubt, she pointed straight ahead... straight at me!

As Luke lifted the blindfold, I narrowed my eyes at her and pulled my lips into a hateful smirk. "Hi Emily," I said, giving her a little wave. Her eyes widened in horror.

"No way," she exclaimed. "No way am I having Ben as my trust buddy. Nope, not gonna happen."

She crossed her arms and stood there indignantly. Luke, having no idea of the history between us, clapped his hands.

"No, no this is the perfect way to end our fantastic afternoon," he said. "You two obviously have some kind of background I don't know about. Probably ex-girlfriend and boyfriend. Am I right?"

"NO!" Emily and I both yelled in unison.

"As if!" said Emily.

"Not if she were the last girl on the

planet," I retaliated.

"OK, OK, I get it," said Luke, holding up his hands. "Whatever you two are, whatever the issue between you is, this is the perfect demonstration of how to build trust. Now, Emily, get yourself on that swing with Elliot. Becky and Ben, you come to the lever. Everyone else watch."

Luke bent down so that he was my height and put his hands on my shoulders, looking me directly in the eye.

"Ben, remember how you felt when you first got on that swing. Scared... terrified even. But you knew that if you needed the swing to stop, all you had to do was shout to your trust buddy and they would make it all end for you. They would stop the swing and make you feel safe again, right?"

"Right," I nodded.

"Good, now you remember that if Emily needs you to make her feel safe OK?"

"OK," I agreed.

What Luke couldn't see was that behind my back, I had my fingers crossed. This was payback time. Payback for everything that my evil arch enemy had done to me in the past. Emily was at my mercy!"

Becky and I gripped the lever together. Then as soon as Luke fastened the straps around the pair, we started to pull it back and forth. Becky was doing it nice and gently, so as to get them gradually used to it. I, on the other hand, decided that it was time to give them an amazing thrill ride. After all, they were the last pair to give it a go. They deserved the best ride ever after waiting all of this time. Well, that's what I told Becky.

Time to scare Evil Emily, I thought to myself.

With an almighty tug, I pulled the lever back so far that Becky's hand flew off of it.

Emily screamed as the swing lurched forward and she suddenly found herself dangling over the cliff edge. Elliot also screamed, but in much more of a *woohoo* way, enjoying every second of his thrill ride.

Emily screamed again as the swing lurched backwards. I could just imagine the feeling in her tummy right now. The feeling that your stomach has somehow jumped out of your body. I remembered that feeling from when I had first started swinging. Then I also remembered the way my legs felt like jelly and how my heart had been racing and my palms were sweaty. Suddenly, I felt guilty. As much as I hated Emily for the things she had done in the past, I couldn't just stand there listening to her terrified noises, knowing that I could help her. I knew I should want to get revenge on her. I knew that Pocket Rocket would relish hearing the details of how I had got my own back on Evil Emily once and for all. But – it just wasn't in my nature. I couldn't do it. I had thought that I wanted to scare her, but when it had come down to it, it hadn't been as much fun as I had expected it be.

Grasping the lever with both hands, I started to steady it and slow the swing down.

"Why's it stopping?" yelled Elliot, disappointed that his thrill ride was coming to a stop. "We only just got started!"

"Don't worry," I shouted back. "I'm just slowing it down to let Emily get used to it. Then she can enjoy it all the more when it goes really high."

I felt a pat on my shoulder and turned around to see Luke smiling at me.

"Good work," he said. "I was just about to slow the swing down myself, but you did good. I'm proud of you."

I smiled at Luke. It sounded like something Dad would say. Something I had always wanted Rob to say. A feeling of warmth replaced the feeling of revenge I had had inside only moments before. It was definitely a feeling I preferred.

Gradually, Emily's screams had stopped, and Becky and I gently sped the swing up until both Elliot and Emily were *woo-hoo'ing* their way through it. It seemed that Emily had crossed the line from fear to exhilaration and I was genuinely happy for her.

CHAPTER 11

"Well, I don't know how you had it in you to be so nice to her after all she's done to you," said Tommy as he plonked himself down on the end of my bunk bed.

It was 9.30pm and we had all been sent to bed about half an hour earlier. We were far too excited to sleep though. Our first day had been amazing and we still had four days left!

"I guess I'm just not as evil as her," I replied. "I did plan on being mean, but it didn't feel as satisfying as I'd expected it to be."

"That's because you're a good person and she's not," said Charlie, joining in the conversation from where he was lying in his bunk bed.

"If the roles had been reversed and it had been you in the swing, Emily would have sabotaged your strap and then pulled so hard on the swing lever that you'd have gone flying off over the cliff top," laughed Ryan.

I shuddered at the thought, thinking that

Ryan was probably only half joking. She hadn't thought twice about trying to break my hand once, so I definitely wouldn't have put it past her.

"Time to go to sleep, boys," said Mr Wallis, poking his head in through the doorway.

Tommy jumped down from my bunk and climbed into his bed.

"Breakfast is at 8am, so I'll come and wake you up just before. Goodnight boys." He turned the light out and zipped up the safari tent door as he left.

"Night, Mr Wallis," we all replied.

I suddenly felt a slight pang of sadness that Mum wasn't there to come and say goodnight. I had been so busy all day that I hadn't given home a second thought. I suddenly remembered the note that I'd hidden under my pillow. I grabbed my torch from next to me and was just about to sneak under my duvet and read it when I was blinded by a light beaming in my face. It was Jayden, shining his torch at me from across the room.

"Anyone up for a game of truth or dare?" he asked mischievously.

"I don't know, I'm actually feeling a bit tired now," said Noah, yawning loudly.

"Don't be such a wet blanket," teased Jayden. "Sleep is for wimps!"

"OK, OK," said Noah. "I'll join in if everyone else does. And, if Ben gives us all some sweets."

"What sweets?" I replied innocently. "We're not allowed sweets here."

"Come on Ben," said Noah. "There's no way you would have come away without your secret school tuck shop stash."

He was, of course, referring to the secret school tuck shop that I had been running ever since I had joined Summercroft School.

"Everyone has been talking about it. I've even brought some spare change with me," he continued, not giving up.

"OK," I relented. "I wasn't planning on making it public knowledge until tomorrow, but yes, I did think it was a business opportunity not to be missed."

I had more than a hundred packets of sweets hidden in the secret compartment of my suitcase, and Tommy had about the same amount in his. We had come away prepared. The teachers had made it very clear that no one was allowed to bring sweets on our trip so we knew we would have a very receptive market. We were going to put our prices up temporarily based on supply and demand. Four nights away from home, and nowhere to buy sweets! The other kids would be more than happy to pay more than usual to get their sugar fix.

Grabbing six mini packets of Haribo from my suitcase, I chucked them at my friends. "These are a freebie as you're my camp mates," I said. "But, as of tomorrow, I will be officially back in business. Just make sure you don't tell the teachers!"

We all sat back up in our beds again, excited for our late night munchies and risky game.

"Let's all shine our torches under our chins so we can see each other," said Tommy. I couldn't see him as he was in the bed under me, but I could see everyone else glowing up in the darkness. I did the same with my torch so that my friends could see my face illuminated in the pitch black tent.

"OK, I'll go first," said Jayden, taking charge. "Charlie, truth or dare?"

"Truth," said Charlie, sounding a little hesitant.

"Have you ever eaten your own earwax?" asked Jayden, giggling.

Shining his own torch brightly in his face, Charlie looked very relieved that Jayden had started him off with such an easy question.

"No," he replied. "I put a big lump of orange earwax to my tongue once, but it tasted really sour and yucky so I flicked it on the floor instead."

"Ew," we all said, laughing.

"Tommy," said Charlie, "truth or dare?"

"Truth," replied Tommy.

"How many bedrooms does your house actually have?" asked Charlie.

Tommy did the cough he always does when he's embarrassed. I didn't need to see him to know how uncomfortable this question made him. He didn't like talking about how rich his parents were after winning the lottery a few years ago, as he thought people would think he was showing off.

"That's a boring question," I said, trying to save my best friend. "Why don't you ask him something interesting, like what's the most cringey thing he's ever done."

"I like the bedroom question," insisted Charlie, not giving up easily. "My mum said she reckons you've got about ten bedrooms. So, how many have you got?"

"I don't know," answered Tommy awkwardly. "Maybe eight or nine."

I heard the other boys in the tent all gasp and say, "wow," in unison.

"Tommy's turn," I said, trying to distract the attention away as I imagined him shifting uncomfortably in his bed.

"Noah," Tommy said quickly, grateful for the swerve ball I had thrown him. "Truth or dare?"

"Truth," replied Noah.

"Why's no one saying 'dare'," moaned Jayden. "It's much more fun if we do dares as well."

"I'll choose a dare on my turn," I said confidently.

"Noah," repeated Tommy, "who do you have a crush on?"

We all made a very annoying 'oooh' sound at this question as Noah blushed red under the torchlight.

"OK, I'll tell you, but only if you promise you won't say anything to anyone," demanded Noah.

"Of course not," said Jayden. "What goes on tour stays on tour."

We all looked at Jayden questioningly. "It's a saying," he explained. "It means that when you're away with a group of friends, anything you do or say has to be kept private and never mentioned again when you get home."

"OK," said Noah. "I guess I quite like Mia."

Mia was a quiet girl from the other class who I hadn't ever really paid any attention to. She obviously hadn't gone unnoticed by Noah though!

"Ben," said Noah. "Truth or dare?"

"Dare," I replied, sticking to my promise to choose a dare on my turn.

"I dare you to run into Mrs Jackson's room and ask if you can sleep in there with her because you're missing your mum!" said Noah.

"No way!" I replied, "I can't do that! What if she says yes and I have to stay in there all night!"

"You said you wanted a dare," said Noah, shrugging.

He was right. Mum always told me that if someone dared you to do something, it was always better to refuse to do it rather than put yourself in danger or do something you'd regret. This wasn't really anything dangerous though. Mrs Jackson would probably just give me a pep talk and send me back to my bed. I could do this.

"Alright, I'll do it," I said boldly.

I climbed down the ladder of my bunk bed and slipped my trainers on over my bare feet. The tent was a bit chilly now the sun had gone down so I was already wearing the cosy onesie Mum had packed for me.

"Let's all go so that we can make sure he doesn't just pretend he's done it," said Jayden. "If we creep along really quietly, no one will see us."

The six of us must have looked a right sight, tip-toeing out of our safari tent in our onesies and trainers. The main accommodation was just a stone's throw away from us so we didn't have far to walk.

"How will we know which room Mrs Jackson is in?" whispered Tommy.

"It's the first one on the left as you go past the living area," said Noah. "I saw her go in there with her suitcase earlier."

I reached up to pull the door handle at the entrance. The warmth hit us as we all sneaked inside. It made us realise that there was a downside to sleeping in the safari tent. We had a chilly night ahead of us whilst the rest of our classmates were tucked up, nice and warm.

"Let's wait here," said Tommy as he crouched down behind a sofa. "We can hear Ben from here without being seen."

I hesitated for a second, momentarily wondering what on earth I was doing. Asking myself *what's the worst that can happen*, and deciding that it wouldn't be too bad, I slowly crept towards the door of Mrs Jackson's bedroom.

Lifting my right hand, I gently tapped my knuckles on the door.

No reply.

I knocked again, this time a little louder.

"Hello," came a sleepy voice from inside. "Is someone there?"

I pulled down on the door handle and opened it just a crack.

"Mrs Jackson," I whispered. "It's me, Ben."

"Is everything OK, Ben?" she asked still sounding half asleep.

"Um, I'm a bit scared Mrs Jackson. And... I'm missing my mum."

I heard muffled laughter coming from the sofa area. Luckily, Mrs Jackson hadn't woken up enough yet to hear it.

"Ah, don't worry love," said Mrs Jackson. "The first night is always a bit strange for everyone."

Well that's a first, I thought to myself. She had never called me 'love' before. Maybe her mothering instincts were kicking in.

"Can I sleep in here with you?" I asked. I nearly choked on the words as I said them, but a dare was a dare!

"Oh dear, Ben," said Mrs Jackson sounding a bit more awake now. "You can't really do that I'm afraid."

Phew. Thank goodness she hadn't said 'yes'. I don't know what I would have done if she'd agreed! Feeling safe in the knowledge that I could retreat back to my safari tent, I decided to give my fellow bunk mates more than they had bargained for.

"Oh, OK," I replied, trying to sound disappointed. "I guess I'll go back to my tent then. But, I'm not sure I'll be able to sleep. I think I know what might help though."

"What's that Ben?" asked Mrs Jackson, sitting up in her bed and switching on the lamp on the bedside table.

I nearly laughed out loud as I saw what she was wearing. I don't know what I had expected her to be wearing to sleep in, but a dog onesie complete with the hood up and floppy ears wasn't the first thing that would have come to mind!

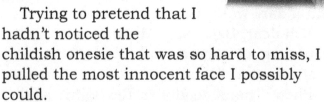

Trying to pretend that I hadn't noticed the childish onesie that was so hard to miss, I pulled the most innocent face I possibly could.

"Well, when I can't sleep at home, my mum always sings me a lullaby."

"Oh, I see," said Mrs Jackson.

"Could you sing me a lullaby please?" I

asked, pulling my eyes wide in an attempt to look vulnerable.

"I don't know Ben. Singing isn't one of my strengths you know."

"That's OK. It's not one of my mum's strengths either." I assured her. "She sounds like a howling cat that's got stuck out in the rain, but it still helps me sleep."

I heard more muffled laughter coming from the sofa and coughed to mask it from Mrs Jackson.

"Well, OK, if it helps," Mrs Jackson reluctantly agreed. "Twinkle twinkle little star, how I won..."

"No, not that one," I said pushing my luck. "Mum always sings me *Dancing Queen* by Abba."

Mrs Jackson looked about the same age

as my mum. It was a pretty safe bet that she liked Abba too. According to Mum they were the best band ever from the 1970's!

"*Dancing Queen* isn't a lullaby Ben," said Mrs Jackson.

"Anything can be a lullaby if you sing it in a soppy voice, Mrs Jackson," I told her in a voice that sounded like butter wouldn't melt. "Please, it really will help me get to sleep."

"OK, if it means you'll go back to bed and let me get my beauty sleep," she relented.

She started singing... "Dancing Queen, young and sweet, only seventeen, oh yeah-eh-eh...you can dance, you can ji-ive, having the time of your li-i-ife, ooh-ooh-ooh-ooh..."

If I had thought Mum was a bad singer, I obviously had never compared her to Mrs Jackson. She sounded like ten howling cats stuck in the rain mixed with twenty screeching hyenas.

The laughter from behind the sofa got louder as my tent mates were unable to contain themselves any longer. I heard them scampering to the door before their laughter gave them away and they were discovered by the teachers. Faced with the realisation that unless I followed them quickly, I'd have to run back to the safari tent on my own in the dark, I decided it was time to bring my dare to an end.

Mrs Jackson was just about to start the second verse when I interrupted her. She actually looked like she was starting to enjoy her impromptu lullaby.

"Thank you so much, Mrs Jackson," I said. "That was just like my mum sings it." I faked a big yawn and stretched my arms up. "I think I'll be able to fall asleep now. Night Mrs Jackson."

"Oh, OK, night Ben. Glad it helped."

As I backed out of the doorway and closed it behind me, I could hear Mrs Jackson humming away to herself. Yep, she definitely liked Abba like my mum. I knew she would.

I raced out of the door after my friends and caught up with them just as they tumbled through the safari tent door. We all collapsed onto our beds breathless with laughter.

"That was brilliant, Ben," exclaimed Ryan in between gasps. "I can't believe you actually got Mrs Jackson to sing to you."

"Well you did send the master to do a dare," I said cockily.

"Now, who's next," I asked, not wanting the game to end. "Jayden, truth or dare?"

CHAPTER 12

We didn't need our wake-up call from Mr Wallis the next morning as the sun started streaming through the canvas of the tent at about 5am, and the birds started their morning chorus. I put a pillow over my head and shut it all out for as long as I could. Eventually, though, I gave up at about 6am when I heard my fellow roommates wriggling around. Momentarily, I wondered if any of my brothers were awake yet back at home.

We had finally fallen asleep at nearly midnight after an eventful game of truth or dare. Thanks to the truth part of the game, we now all knew that Jayden's favourite part of his body was his belly button, and that Charlie's most embarrassing childhood memory was letting his big sister dress him up as a girl and push him around in a toy buggy.

Unfortunately, everyone also now knew that I had once eaten a dog biscuit and actually enjoyed it so much that I had eaten another seven before my dad had realised what I was doing and snatched the packet from me. The most embarrassing part was that I hadn't even been a clueless toddler at the time. It was when I was eight!

No one was able to match the brilliance of my dare with Mrs Jackson, but it had been highly entertaining to see Tommy smell one of Ryan's dirty socks for ten seconds and Noah run outside shouting, "I believe in fairies," three times whilst clapping his hands. The plan had been to tell the teacher who found him that he was sleep walking but not a single one of them stirred, much to our disappointment.

Two dares still needed carrying out today, and I for one was very much looking forward to seeing them.

"Time to draw on your tummy!" I said to Tommy, dropping my head down over the side of my bunk bed. Tommy groaned at me and pulled his pillow over his head.

"Truth or dare finished last night, Ben," he said, hoping for a way out. "The moment's passed."

"Nice try," I replied. "You're not getting out of it that easily." I turned to Jayden. "Have you got that black marker pen you said you had?"

"No way, not a marker pen!" said Tommy.

"Alright, just a felt tip pen then," I said, feeling kind.

I jumped down from my bed and grabbed my pencil case from my drawer. Tommy reluctantly climbed out of his bed and lifted his top up. Kneeling down in front of him. I started to draw some eyes, eyebrows, and a nose just above his belly button. Tommy squidged his belly button together and said "Have a nice day, Ben."

We all started laughing at that, including Tommy.

"That looked so real!" exclaimed Jayden. "It was like your stomach was actually a talking face!"

"How many people did we say he has to

do it to?" asked Charlie.

"Either ten children or one teacher," Ryan said. "It's your choice, Tommy."

"I'll decide after breakfast," said Tommy. Luckily he was starting to see the funny side of his dare. "Don't forget about Noah's dare too," he reminded us.

After opting for a dare at the end of our game last night, Tommy had dared Noah to hug every tree he saw the following day. Noah had negotiated it down to twelve trees, which made sense as otherwise he would end up hugging the entire forest!

We all got dressed and wandered over to the main accommodation just before 8am to see what was for breakfast. We were met with a mass array of cereal, toast, eggs, croissants, and even some pancakes. The rumours about the food being amazing here were one hundred percent accurate.

The rest of the day involved bushcraft taught by the Komodo Camp guys. I was in a group of ten, led by Luke. There was a bit of a hairy moment when Mia singed her eyebrows on the camp fire we had made,

but apart from that it all went pretty smoothly. As well as learning how to make a flame, Luke taught us how to spot animal tracks and make a camp that would protect us from wind and rain. He even told us which bugs we could eat and how you could drink your own wee if you didn't have any clean water. Not surprisingly, none of us fancied testing this out!

Tommy was in my group too and saw his chance to get his dare out of the way on Luke rather than embarrassing himself with an actual teacher. Just as Luke told us it was time to head back to camp, Tommy lifted up his top and gave his tummy a good squidge, saying, "Have a nice evening" to Luke as we walked past. The whole group erupted into laughter as Tommy walked on as if nothing had happened. He had carried out his dare with style and grace.

CHAPTER 13

"I'm not sure it technically counts as completing your dare," Charlie said, looking at Tommy.

We were all lying in our bunk beds chatting about our day before going to sleep.

"We did say ten kids or one teacher, and Luke isn't technically a teacher," joined in Noah.

"But he is an adult," I said. "And he was teaching us stuff, so he kind of was a teacher today."

The others reluctantly nodded their heads in agreement, letting Tommy off the hook.

Jayden and Charlie had confirmed that Noah had hugged not just twelve trees whilst doing their bushcraft lessons, but fifteen trees! According to Noah he had just lost count, but the others thought that he had actually done it out of choice after starting to enjoy the whole experience!

I was just about to ask him what was so good about it when there was a tapping at the door.

"What's the password?" I said in a loud whisper.

Earlier in the day, we had spread the word around about the secret school camp tuck shop. Anyone who wanted to buy something from it had to sneak to the safari tent after the teachers had gone to bed and say the password.

"Yellow pear drops," came the reply.

"You may enter," I responded.

The zip on our safari tent door opened and three girls entered – Sophia, Mollie, and Mia.

Noah went bright red when he saw Mia, remembering his confession from our truth or dare night.

"Your eyebrows look good Mia," Jayden said laughing. "I heard the singed look is all the rage at the moment."

"Shut up," snapped Mia, glaring at him.

It would appear that she wasn't quite ready to see the funny side of her little mishap!

"Ew, why does it smell of wee in here?" exclaimed Mollie, screwing up her face in disgust.

"That'll be our wee bucket," Charlie said matter of factly.

"I didn't think anyone had used it," I said in surprise. I sniffed the air and noticed for the first time that the tent was a little bit whiffy.

"I used it last night," admitted Tommy.

"So did I," said Charlie.

"Me too," said Jayden.

"Did none of you think to empty it?" Mollie asked in horror. "It must be nearly over-flowing with boy wee!"

"Why did you say *boy wee*?" I asked. "Wee is wee."

"Boy wee smells worse," said Mollie, as her two friends nodded their agreement.

"That's so stupid," said Jayden.

"So, what can we do for you ladies?" I said, as if I didn't already know.

"Don't pretend like you don't know, Ben," said the ever-confident Sophia. "We've heard the rumour about your secret tuck shop. How else would we have known the password to use?"

"OK," I reassured her. "I'm just messing. What would you like? I've got soft mints, Haribo, strawberry laces and some packs of Fruitella."

"Haven't you got any chocolate?" asked Mia. "I really need some chocolate tonight."

"Oh," I nodded, pointing to my eyebrows. "Is that like comfort food because of the eyebrow situation?"

"Shut up, Ben," said Mia, glaring at me.

Jeez, these girls were so sensitive!

"Sorry, no chocolate here," I said. "It's been so hot, we thought it would just melt."

"OK, I'll have a packet of Haribo then please," said Sophia, handing me a one pound coin.

I reached into my clothes drawer and pulled out a mini packet of Haribo.

"Ew, this smells of boys' socks," moaned Sophia as she snatched it. "And it's tiny." "How can you charge a pound for this?"

"Supply and demand," I replied arrogantly. "If you see anywhere else around here that you can get it cheaper, then be my guest."

Knowing that I was literally their only chance of getting a sugar fix, Sophia reluctantly relented. Mia and Mollie both chose mints and handed over their pound coins. The mints didn't make quite as good profit as the packet of Haribo but I still made at least 30p on each packet. Charging £1 for everything in the secret tuck shop made sense as I knew that parents had been advised to give their kids ten £1 coins for spending money on the trip.

The girls snuck their sweets up their sleeves, just in case they bumped into an unsuspecting teacher on their way back to bed.

"Bye girls, pleasure doing business with you," I said as they stepped through the door.

"How much have you made now?" asked Jayden.

"£3," I replied. "They were our first customers. "I'm sure there'll be more as word spreads. Anyway, who's going to empty the wee bucket?"

Five minutes later, Charlie traipsed out of the door with the bucket sloshing as he went. Unfortunately for him, Jayden and Tommy had both beaten him in an arm wrestling competition to decide who the unlucky bucket cleaner would be.

Just as he walked back in, there was another knock at the door. This time it was Tommy who shouted, "What's the password?"

The next half an hour saw a steady stream of kids sneaking in to buy their sweets. They then would creep back to the main block and secretly eat them under the covers of their beds, whilst the teachers slept blissfully unaware.

When the last customers of the night left, I stretched my arms up and gave a big yawn as I climbed into my top bunk. £3 profit had very quickly turned into £25. Nice!

As I lay my head down on the pillow, my mind wandered to thoughts of my family. I had been so busy during the day that I had barely had a chance to miss them. It was different at night though. Lying in my unfamiliar bed made me feel a little homesick. I turned on my side trying not to get upset and heard a little crinkle. I suddenly remembered again the letter that Mum had snuck into my suitcase. I waited until I was sure all my roommates were fast asleep and then pulled the envelope out. Shining my torch on it, I opened it up and slid out the piece of paper that was inside. I immediately felt comforted at the sight of Mum's handwriting.

Dear Ben, I hope you're having an amazing time at camp! I won't get all soppy as know you'll tell me off but I just wanted to tell you we're all missing you loads. I've hidden some flapjacks for you in your suitcase for you to share with Tommy as a midnight feast. There's a secret compartment at the bottom if you lift the flap up. Sneaky, hey!

Please don't get in any trouble like running a

secret camp tuck shop or anything like that! And remember, if you do play truth or dare, it's ok to say 'No' to a dare if it's dangerous.

Lots of love and hugs, Mum... P.S. Don't forget to put fresh pants and socks on every morning, and maybe take at least one shower whilst you're there!

I chuckled to myself as I read it. Mum was so predictable. I could have pretty much guessed everything she had written in there. Except for the flapjacks bit! I hadn't noticed a secret compartment in the case. I momentarily considered jumping down to take a look but tiredness won out and I couldn't bring myself to climb out of bed. The flapjacks would keep until tomorrow.

CHAPTER 14

The following morning, we were the first to breakfast again, thanks to the early morning light and the birds waking us. The other kids all piled in to grab their breakfast shortly after. Everyone was chatting away, excited to see what we were going to be doing today. We didn't have to wait long as Mr Wallis clapped his hands together to get our attention.

"I hope you all had a good night's sleep, kids, because today you are going to be doing some orienteering!" he said enthusiastically.

"You will start off here and find your way through the forest, following clues that will take you to checkpoints and eventually get you to a secret meeting point. Any questions?"

Maisie put her hand up.

"Yes, Maisie," said Mr Wallis.

"How are we meant to do that when you told us not to bring our phones? None of us have googlemaps."

Mr Wallis rolled his eyes. "People haven't

always had electronic gadgets to get them from A to B Maisie. You're going to have to navigate your way around the forest just like people would have done a few years back. You're going to be using a good old-fashioned compass!"

"A what?" asked Maisie, looking confused.

"A compass!" said Mr Wallis, widening his eyes. "Surely you've heard of a compass, kids!"

Lots of faces stared blankly back at him.

"Can anyone explain what a compass is? Anyone... anyone at all?" he asked hopefully.

I didn't want to look like a know-it-all, but I put my hand up along with a couple of other kids.

"Yes, Ben," said Mr Wallis, looking

relieved. "Please can you enlighten your fellow classmates?"

"It's a little round thing with magnets in it that always points to the north so you know which direction you're walking in," I told him. I had seen it on a documentary with Dad once. Mum had gone out for the night and all of my brothers had been in bed. It was a programme about a guy who'd been in the SAS. He was dropped by helicopter in the middle of a jungle and had to find his way out using just his survival skills and a compass. A bit like we were doing now, but with the added risk of poisonous snakes and tigers wanting to eat him.

"Correct Ben," confirmed Mr Wallis. "We're going to split you up into ten groups of six. As I said, you'll have a compass, and judging by the blank faces that looked at me just minutes ago, I think it would be a good idea to give you all a quick lesson on how to use it before we go."

I was put in a group with Tommy, Maisie, Jayden, Chloe, and Sophia who I had shared the adrenaline rush swing with yesterday. I was more than happy with this group. Sophia was obviously not scared of a bit of danger, and I had my best friend Tommy with me. Perfect.

About an hour later, after lots of faffing around making sure everyone understood how to use their compass, my group nominated me as the leader and we set off to the forest. Mr Skills was just outside the door, giving another group some advice. My competitive gene came out as I quickened my pace. Mr Wallis had said that the first group back got a prize, and I intended that group to be mine.

CHAPTER 15

"We should give ourselves a team name," said Sophia. "Like, the Rambling Rangers, or, the Awesome Adventurers, or something like that."

"How about the Wishful Wanderers?" said Tommy.

"Let's have a vote," suggested Maisie. "Hands up for the Rambling Rangers."

Chloe put her hand up.

"Hands up for the Awesome Adventures," continued Maisie.

She put her own hand up along with Sophia.

"Hands up for the Wishful Wanderers?"

Tommy, Jayden and I all put our hands up.

"Looks like the Wishful Wanderers" is the winner," I said.

"That's not fair," said Maisie. "You all stuck together coz you're all boys!"

"That wasn't the reason," I replied. "It was just the better name." If I was being completely honest, the name was a bit rubbish. It made me think of people walking around the forest in a trance like state, soaking up the wonder of nature, not a team of kids on a quest to fight for first place in an orienteering mission. But Tommy had chosen it and I had to support my best friend.

"We don't have to choose that one," said Tommy. He always tried to avoid conflict where possible. "It was a bit of a lame name. What about the Tremendous Trekkers instead?"

"Hmm, I do quite like that one actually," said Maisie after thinking for a few seconds. "What does everyone else think?"

"What's a 'trekker'," asked Jayden, looking confused.

"Someone who makes a long, hard journey," Tommy explained.

I had to admit, it was a better name, and Tommy had still been the one to choose it. We all nodded in agreement.

"That's decided then," said Maisie. "We are the team Tremendous Trekkers!"

With that decided, we carried on our walk into the forest in search of our first clue. Mr Skills had told us that the task should take around three hours from start to finish. We all had our own backpacks with a bottle of water and a pack lunch, and had been given strict instructions not to eat it until we'd been walking for at least a couple of hours.

Our first clue, given to us by Mr Skills was, *'Standing tall and majestic in your path, I'm wearing a red ribbon. From here, I will give you directions for which you will need your compass. P.S. You may hug me if you like.'*

"So, if we keep walking down this path, we'll bump into someone wearing a red ribbon," said Sophia. "That sounds easy enough."

We set off down the path together, excited to be starting our adventure. The groups had been staggered so that we didn't all set off at the same time and follow each other. Mr Skills recorded the time we all departed so that the winning team was a true representation of time taken, rather than who got there first. I was still glad that we were the first to leave though. I liked the feeling of being in front.

"Who do you think it will be?" asked Jayden.

"I reckon it'll be Luke who helped us on the swing yesterday," I said. "I'm not sure why he'd say we can all give him a hug though. That's a bit strange."

"Or maybe it'll be Mrs Jackson so that she can check we're all OK," said Maisie. "They must be a bit worried about us all heading into the forest without any grown-ups."

"I don't think it's as big as you think," I replied. "My mum looked this place up on their website before we came, and in the parents' section it told parents not to worry about the orienteering bit as the forest is actually all cordoned off with fencing to stop us wandering off too far."

"Ah, that makes sense," said Maisie.

"Besides," I said. "The Isle of Wight isn't that big. How lost could we get?"

"Yeah, we'll be fine," agreed Tommy. "I reckon we'll have this done and dusted in half the time they've said."

Feeling confident, we quickened our pace in search of someone wearing a red ribbon. After about five minutes, Sophia started laughing as she ran up ahead.

"Look," she shouted. "It wasn't a person

after all. "It's a tree that's wearing the ribbon! The *'you can give me a hug'* part of the clue was referring to hippies who like to hug trees."

"Or Noah," Tommy said, giggling. "He'd be a natural at this after yesterday!"

He was, of course, referring to Noah's dare from the other night where he had to hug twelve trees.

"What are you talking about?" asked Chloe.

Tommy, Jayden and I looked at each other. "Nothing," the three of us said in unison.

As Jayden said on our first night, what goes on tour, stays on tour.

A piece of paper had been stuck on to the ribbon that had been tied around the massive trunk of the tree. The tree must have been hundreds of years old. Sophia stretched her arms around it to give it a hug and they didn't even make it half-way round!

"This actually feels quite relaxing," Sophia said. "You guys should try it."

The other girls all moved towards the tree and copied her.

"You know you lot look like you're crazy, don't you?" I said to them.

"Don't mock us until you've tried it," said Maisie. "Sophia's right, it does make you feel relaxed."

"Alright, move out of the way then," I said. I could handle hugging the tree but didn't want to risk accidentally hugging any of the girls as well!

I wrapped my arms as far as I could around the tree. As I did, I felt a wave of calm come over me. Mum had once told me that hugging a tree helped you to relax – something about reconnecting with nature.

At the time I'd thought she was mad but maybe it wasn't so crazy after all. I hugged the tree for maybe a few more seconds than I intended to.

"See!" exclaimed Maisie, feeling triumphant. "I told you it's relaxing."

"OK, maybe a tiny bit," I said, not wanting to admit I was wrong.

"OK, as lovely as this is," said Jayden, "hugging trees, is not going to win us this race. Let's read the note and find the next landmark."

"Ok," said Sophia, reading the note on the tree.

"Using your compass, take one hundred steps on an angle of one hundred and thirty degrees."

Lifting up the compass that I had tied around my neck, I laid it flat on my hand in front of my chest. With the magnetic needle pointing north, I twisted the direction needle to 130 degrees. "We need to head this way," I said to everyone. "Let's go Tremendous Trekkers!"

Confident in my ability, the team followed me in the direction the compass had told me to go. This was going to be easy!

CHAPTER 16

"Look, there it is!" shouted Tommy, charging ahead of us.

Sure enough, in the distance stood another tree with a red ribbon wrapped around it. A note was attached.

Tommy read it out to us as we all joined him. "Congratulations on making it to checkpoint two! Now take eighty steps in a ninety-degree direction, but beware of the stream and work as a team!"

"Ooh, that sounds fun," said Sophia. "I wonder if we'll need to make a raft to cross it."

"It said a stream, Sophia," I said in an annoying know-it-all way. "Not a river. We probably just need to cross over where there are some logs or something."

"Or I could lay down across it and you could all walk over me?" Jayden said, selflessly. He was easily the tallest of us.

"Sounds like a plan," I said. "Let's walk quickly before the other teams catch us up."

Feeling like a bit of an expert with the compass now, I led the way through the forest to the next checkpoint. The tree line was getting denser now as we headed deeper into the forest. It was another hot day, and I was glad of the shade created by the tree canopy above us.

It didn't take us long to walk eighty steps, and we soon came to a stream trickling across the path in front of us.

"That doesn't look too deep," said Chloe. "We could probably just walk in it."

"Don't be fooled," I told her. "It's probably deeper than it looks. "Let's test it with this stick."

I picked up a stick and put it into the stream. Sure enough, it went deeper than Chloe had thought. Not deep enough to swim, but deep enough to go over the tops of our trainers and give us soggy feet for the rest of the day.

"OK, so we need to either find a log long enough to stretch over it, or all walk over Jayden," said Chloe.

Jayden didn't look so keen on the idea of everyone walking on him now it was actually a reality! "Um, maybe let's see if we can find some logs first," he said. "Then, if we can't, I'll make myself into a human bridge."

We all spent the next ten minutes gathering branches from around us, but none of them quite reached the other side. I suddenly remembered passing a small tree that had fallen down a little way back along the path. If we all worked as a team, we should be able to lift it.

Suggesting my idea to the Tremendous Trekkers, we ran back down the path in the direction we had come from, eager to keep our lead over the other teams.

"There it is!" I shouted, spotting the fallen tree. All six of us positioned ourselves along the length of the trunk.

"Everyone lift on the count of three," I said. "One, two, three!"

We all heaved upwards with as much strength as we could muster. Alone, there was no way in the world I could have done it, but as a team, the tree lifted with ease.

We traipsed back along the path with our tree and laid it down across the stream, standing back to admire our efforts.

"Who's going to test it out?" asked Maisie, looking a little concerned.

"I will," said Sophia.

I wasn't surprised, given that she had been the first to put her hand up to try the adrenaline swing with me. She reminded me a bit of a girl called Amy who I had met the summer before. Amy taught me some really cool skateboarding tricks whilst staying with her grandad who lived up the road from me.

"Argh, it's a bit wobbly," said Sophia as she put her arms out to balance herself. "Can you guys sit on it or something to steady it?"

The five of us straddled our legs over the tree and sat down.

Our weight helped to stop the tree from shaking and Sophia walked along it to the other side of the stream with ease. We all clapped and whooped as she stepped off the other side.

"Come on you lot, it's easy!" she said, feeling chuffed with herself.

We all took it in turns to get up from our seated positions and walk along the tree. Tommy was the next to go, then Chloe, then Maisie, then Jayden. I was the last one as I was sitting at the end of the tree. Once Jayden had made it across to the other side, I stood up to take my turn. The tree trunk wobbled as I stepped onto it. "Whoa!" I exclaimed. "It's gone all wobbly again now that there's no one left to sit on it for me!"

"But I thought you were a black belt in karate," challenged Sophia. "Doesn't that mean you should have good balance?"

She was right. I engaged my stomach muscles and put my arms out to help me steady myself. Fixing my gaze on the end of the tree trunk I put one foot in front of the other. My confident stance stopped the tree shaking, and with a couple of steps I had made it to the other side. Everyone clapped and whooped some more. I smiled at my fellow Tremendous Trekkers feeling lucky that they had been chosen to be part of my team.

We started walking again when Chloe suddenly stopped us. "You know we've done all the hard work," she said. "All the teams that get here after us are just going to walk straight over the log that we've laid down."

"That doesn't seem fair," said Maisie. She had a mischievous glint in her eye. "We could always pull the tree over to this side with us," she said. "That way, everyone else will have to find their own way over, just like we did."

"It seems a bit mean," said Tommy. "The tree is there anyway now. We may as well let everyone use it."

I put my hands on my best friend's shoulders and looked him in the eye. "Tommy," I said. "There is a time to be nice, and there is a time to be competitive. Moving the tree isn't mean... it's necessary."

"He's right," agreed Sophia as she

followed me back to the stream. "Let's do this."

The majority of the tree trunk was right over on the other side so it wasn't going to be easy. I grabbed on to the end of it and Sophia wrapped her arms around my waist. Chloe then held on to her, and Maisie and Jayden followed suit. Tommy reluctantly brought up the end of our human train. An image of one of Little Spud's books flashed up into my head where a farmer and his wife and all of their animals heaved a gigantic turnip up out of the ground.

We all tugged as hard as we could until gradually the tree trunk slid across the stream towards us. It made a splash as the end of it dropped into the cool water, feeling satisfyingly refreshing as it splattered my face.

With a few more tugs we had got it completely over onto our side and we all collapsed to the ground panting.

"Good work Tremendous Trekkers," I told my team.

Just then, we heard voices coming towards us. The time it had taken us to mess around with the tree had given the next team time to catch us up.

"Hey!" shouted a voice I recognised only too well as Evil Emily. "That's not fair!"

"Sorry Emily," I said, shrugging my shoulders at her. "Life isn't fair sometimes."

"Don't get your feet wet!" giggled Sophia as we all turned to carry on our adventure, high-fiving each other as we went.

Tommy turned his head back to Emily and her team. "I think I saw another tree you could use a bit further back," he started to say. The rest of us grabbed him, laughing. He really didn't possess the competitive gene my brothers and I had inherited.

CHAPTER 17

We completed the next six stages with ease, keeping a comfortable lead ahead of all the other teams. We must have been walking for about an hour and a half when the forest suddenly turned very still. The bright sunshine that had been glinting through the trees disappeared as everything turned gloomy. I could hear a low rumble in the distance.

"Did anyone else just hear that?" Maisie asked looking worried.

"Yep," I responded, as we all nodded our heads to confirm that we too had heard the ominous sound of thunder.

"Don't worry though," I said. "I'm sure it's nowhere near us. Let's wait for the lightning and then count to see how many miles away it is."

"Oh yeah," said Sophia. "I did that with my dad once. When the lightning flashes, you start counting, and every second you count means the thunder storm is one mile away."

"Yeah, but it's not one second to one

mile," I said. "Everyone thinks that, but it's actually five seconds for every one mile."

"He's right," said Chloe, looking apologetically at Sophia. "They taught us how to do it at Brownie camp last year. Every five seconds is one mile. And you have to count properly, like *one elephant, two elephant, three elephant*, so you don't go too fast."

"OK," relented Sophia. "Let's try it then.

We all stood still waiting for a bolt of lightning to appear. A few seconds passed. Nothing! A few more seconds passed. Still nothing.

"You know, we could be waiting here for ages," said Jayden. "I bet it was just a little storm in the distance that's already gone out to sea."

"You're right," I agreed. "Let's keep walking before all the other teams catch us up."

Scampering away into the forest that had so quickly become several shades darker, we all hoped that I was right.

Unfortunately though, this was one of the rare occasions that I wasn't right. In fact, I couldn't have been more wrong.

Just moments later, the heavens opened as enormous droplets of rain came lashing down on us. Within seconds, we were soaked through. The darkened forest suddenly glowed bright as though a lightbulb had been switched on as lightning flashed somewhere above the trees. We all started counting.

"One elephant, two elephant, three elephant, four elephant..."

We didn't make it to five. We all jumped out of our skin as a huge clap of thunder burst out above us. A collective scream escaped from our lips.

"I know maths isn't my strong point," said Jayden. "But, by my calculations, that storm isn't even one mile away!"

"Isn't it dangerous to be outside in a storm?" asked Tommy to no one in particular.

"I think it's exciting," said Sophia, holding her arms out and tipping her face up towards the sky.

"Tommy's right," I said. "I once ran outside to see a storm when I was little and I'll never forget my mum dragging me in and saying *'when thunder roars, stay indoors.'* You can literally get struck by the lightning."

"The chances of that happening are one in five hundred thousand," argued Sophia.

"You have more chance of being killed by an asteroid!"

I made a mental note to look up the chances of being killed by an asteroid when I got home to see if she was right. She sounded pretty convincing.

"All the same," Tommy said. "I think we should take shelter until the storm passes... just in case."

Maisie and Chloe nodded in agreement. I wanted to agree with my friend, but all I could hear was the niggly voice in my head telling me to keep our lead ahead of the other groups.

"Let's take a vote," I shouted over the pounding rain as another crack of thunder boomed overhead. "Hands up if you want to take shelter."

Maisie, Chloe and Tommy all put their hands up.

"And, hands up who wants to keep going?"

Myself, Jayden, and Sophia all shot our hands up without a moment's hesitation. I guess the divide between those of us possessing the competitive gene had been decided.

"Fifty-fifty," I said. "Which means that the team leader gets to decide – in other words me! Let's keep going Tremendous Trekkers. We've got this in the bag!"

Heading up a team of three excited trekkers and three reluctant trekkers, we started to navigate our way up a path. Before the storm, we wouldn't have noticed how steep it was. What was once a nice solid path however, had now become a slippery mud bath. Maisie started to trail behind as she struggled to hold her grip. I had an idea.

"You guys keep going," I shouted to my team mates as I walked back past them, handing Tommy the compass. "I'll help Maisie."

I would say that I was being purely selfless and quote the *'a friend in need is a friend indeed'* line to you but, if I was being perfectly honest, I just didn't want her to slow us down and make us miss out on being first to the finish!

I had to move carefully past my friends as there was a sharp drop to edge of the path which would, at best, add another half an hour to my journey time clambering back up it if I fell down, and at worst probably break my leg!

"Grab onto my bag strap," I said to Maisie as I reached her. She looked up at me miserably. Her hair was slicked over her forehead and her clothes were sticking to her skin as she battled in the rain.

Doing as she was told, I heaved her along behind me, forcing her to quicken her pace. Suddenly, there was a massive crack of thunder right above us, even louder than the others we had heard. A creaking noise followed and I stopped dead in my tracks as my eyes widened in horror. Before I knew what was happening, a tree had come crashing down in front of me as lightning struck it.

Maisie and I jerked ourselves backwards to avoid being hit, but the ground was too slippery to hold us. Losing our footing, we stumbled to the left. I felt myself being tugged backwards where Maisie was still gripping tightly to my bag. The next few seconds were a blur as we tumbled head over heels down the steep slope, eventually coming to rest in a thicket of dense bushes.

I shook my head trying to overcome the

dizziness that I felt, when I realised that Maisie was no longer holding onto my bag.

"Maisie," I yelled, unable to see her. There was no reply. "MAISIE," I shouted again, more urgently this time.

I breathed a sigh of relief as I heard her reply. "Ben! I'm over here. I can't move."

Following the sound of her voice, I pushed through the bushes and saw that she had come to a stop about five metres away from me. Her face was grimacing with pain.

"I think I've broken my ankle," she said.

I looked down and saw that her ankle was bent at a very awkward angle. It definitely looked broken.

"Nah, that's not broken," I lied. "Just a little twisted, that's all. You'll be fine."

She didn't look convinced but managed a little weak smile through her tears.

"All you need to do is lean on me and I'll help you back up this slope. Then we can all take it in turns to give you piggy backs to the finish. How does that sound?" I said, sounding more confident with my plan than I felt. "Now after three, I'm going to pull you up. Ready? One, two three."

Maisie shrieked as I failed dismally to pull her to her feet. She collapsed back down into the bushes. She must be heavier than she looked.

"Blimey, how much do you weigh?" I asked, rubbing my sore back. I had made it through the fall with just a few scrapes and bruises, but pulling Maisie up off the ground had nearly broken my back!

She stared at me for a second and then broke into floods of tears. Oops! Dad had once told me never to tell a girl she was heavy under any circumstances. This was obviously why.

"Erm, sorry," I said realising my mistake. "I think my arms must be weak from the fall." *Nice recovery*, I thought to myself. "Let's try again."

This time, I braced myself better and pulled on Maisie with both hands. With a bit of effort, I managed to get her to her feet where she balanced precariously on her uninjured one.

"Now, hold on to my bag like you were

before," I said, "and I'll just pull you up this hill so we can catch up with the others."

Maisie sniffed and wiped her nose on her sleeve as she tried to compose herself. Another loud crack of thunder made us both jump, reminding us of the force of nature that had put us in this predicament. Suddenly, I heard voices above us.

"Ben! Maisie! Where are you?"

It was Tommy and the other Tremendous Trekkers. They had come back for us!

"We're down here!" I yelled back.

"Are you both OK?" shouted a voice that I recognised as Chloe's. "We heard screaming."

"Yep, we're OK." I shouted back. "Maisie has brok..." I started to say, but quickly caught myself when I saw Maisie's startled face. "Twisted her ankle," I finished. "But I'm pulling her up. We'll be there in a minute."

It would seem that I was being a little bit optimistic though. After clawing my way half way up the treacherous hill, digging my trainers into the sodden ground, the weight of both of us became too much and we slid right back to where we had started.

"This is useless," Maisie cried, clutching her ankle in pain.

She was right. I'd be able to make it up the slope if I was on my own, but there was no way I could pull Maisie up there, too. I had two choices...

1. Snap off a nice big leaf for Maisie to use as an umbrella and wish her luck as I scampered up the hill to safety, or...

2. Stay with Maisie and keep her safe until help arrived.

It was a tough call but I decided to do the right thing and go for number two.

"We can't do it," I shouted. "You need to

go and get help!"

"OK, we'll get to the end as quickly as we can and find the teachers," shouted Tommy.

"Are we going be stuck out here all night?" sobbed Maisie.

"No," I replied, more confidently than I felt. "Tommy and the others will show the teachers where we are and they'll come and rescue us. Maybe they'll even bring a helicopter to pull us out!" I joked.

"We're not in an episode of *Fireman Sam*," said Maisie, raising her eyebrows up at me.

"It feels a bit like we are," I said, laughing.

"So move aside, make away,
It's Fireman Ben
He's gonna save the day,
It's Fireman Ben..." I sang.

"Erm Ben, did you hit your head when you fell down the hill?" Maisie asked, looking concerned.

"Only a couple of times," I answered, stopping mid-song. "Why?"

"'Coz, we're lying here trapped in the middle of the forest, in a thunder storm, and you're singing *Fireman Sam,*" she said.

"Only, apparently, you are the Fireman, not Sam." Again she raised her eyebrows at me.

For someone who was in pain with a broken ankle, she could certainly bring on the sarcasm!

"I was just trying to cheer you up," I said, pushing my hand through my hair like I always did when I was embarrassed. I sometimes sang *Fireman Sam* to Big Spud and Little Spud when they pretended to get their toys stuck up a tree at home. I would then climb the tree like the brave big brother I am and rescue the teddies. I hadn't even realised I was singing it until Maisie had mentioned it. Maybe I had hit my head a bit harder than I realised. I felt around it for lumps and winced as I felt a sore bump just above my left ear.

"OK, so how about you don't tell anyone about me singing Fireman Sam," I said, "and I won't tell anyone how you peed your pants with fear when you fell down the hill?"

Maisie went bright red. "It was only a little bit of wee!" she exclaimed. "And it was really scary!"

Oh wow. I'd only been bluffing. I didn't realise she had actually peed her pants!

"OK, so shall we keep each other's secrets then," I asked, holding out my pinky finger.

Maisie reluctantly linked her pinky finger into mine, looking embarrassed.

"OK," she said. "What happens in the forest stays in the forest."

CHAPTER 18

The loud claps of thunder reduced to a slow rumble as the storm moved away. The rain stopped almost as suddenly as it had started, and the sun once again beamed its rays through the trees, as if reappearing after a game of hide and seek.

Initially, we expected to hear the voices of our other classmates up above us as they continued with their orienteering mission. We soon came to the realisation, though that they had all had the sense to turn back when the storm had started and were probably back at the camp wrapped in cosy blankets, sipping hot chocolate.

"We've been sitting here for ages," moaned Maisie as she put down the leaf umbrella that I had made her out of some ferns. "What if they can't remember the way back to us?"

"Don't worry," I reassured her. "The teachers know the route we took. They'll be here any minute now."

I sounded more convinced than I actually felt. I didn't have a watch on but it definitely felt like we had been stuck down here for at least an hour.

"How's your ankle feeling?" I asked Maisie.

"Um, let me see," said Maisie. "Like I fell down a hill and snapped it in two after some idiot wouldn't listen to my suggestion to take shelter during the storm!" she spat out at me.

"So it's a little bit sore then?" I replied sarcastically.

"Yes, Ben, it is a lot bit sore!" she said through clenched teeth.

"*A lot bit sore* doesn't really make sense," I told her.

"Do you really think now is the time to be playing grammar police?" she demanded as her nostrils flared out.

She had a point. Correcting someone's grammar was annoying at the best of times. I often did it to Mum when she got herself in a fluster, telling us off for something. For some reason, it always made her even madder when I pointed out her grammatical mistakes!

"Sorry Maisie," I said. "And sorry I dragged you along in the thunder storm.

I know this is all my fault."

"Yes, it is," she huffed, folding her arms like Little Spud did whenever he was in a strop.

We both sat in silence for a few minutes.

"Do you want me to tell you a joke to cheer you up?

"No,"

"OK, but you're missing out, trust me."

"OK... but it had better be good, or I'm not laughing."

Wow, she was a tough customer.

"What do you call a man who irons clothes?"

Maisie raised her eyebrows at me.

"Iron man," I said.

She didn't laugh.

"That is so not funny Ben."

OK, I guess I needed to up my game.

"Why is Peter Pan always flying?

"I don't know," she puffed. "Why is Peter Pan always flying?"

"Because he never lands!"

I paused, waiting for her to laugh.

Still nothing. Not even the slightest of giggles! I decided to give it one last shot and use the joke Pocket Rocket had told me last week.

"An old lady at the bank asked me to help her check her balance... so, I pushed her over."

Maisie made a very unusual snorting noise, followed by a little chuckle, followed by a loud gasping of breath, followed by proper belly laughter with tears rolling down her cheeks! I think you could safely say that my joke had hit the spot. Maisie's laughter was contagious and soon, I was laughing too.

When she finally caught her breath, she said. "It wasn't that funny."

"You liar!" I exclaimed. "You nearly peed your pants again, you were laughing so much."

For a second, her eyes bore into mine like lasers, but then, much to my relief, she started laughing again.

"OK, OK, it was funny."

"It was," I agreed. "But I think you are a bit delirious from the pain in your ankle too. Maybe we should prop it up a bit to support it."

I grabbed a bunch of fern from next to me and molded it into a ball shape as best I could. Gently lifting Maisie's leg up, I wedged it underneath her ankle as she winced.

"Sorry," I said.

"I'm sorry too," she said. "It wasn't your fault. I shouldn't have said that. I just took it out on you because my ankle hurts."

"That's OK," I said. "I'm used to getting the blame for everything. I have three little brothers remember?"

"Oh yeah," she giggled. "Tell me some of the naughty stuff Little Spud has done lately to take my mind off my ankle."

Everyone had heard of my youngest brother's antics. He was practically famous where we lived, and we'd only been there for one year!

"OK, well we nearly had him here with us instead of my clothes," I started, as I told her about Little Spud's attempt to sneak in my suitcase.

"Oh, and he nearly got me disqualified from my karate tournament by attacking my opponent!" I continued.

"And last week, he pulled a live fish out of his fish tank and dissected it," I finished.

147

Maisie gasped. "No way! That's so mean."

"I know," I agreed. "He's just really interested in how stuff works," I said, feeling like I had to justify it somehow. "He was so upset when he realised the fish was dead."

"He sounds worse than my little sister," said Maisie. "She cut big chunks of her own hair last week and when I laughed at her, she grabbed the scissors and cut mine too!"

I chuckled as I acknowledged Maisie's shorter haircut! "I thought it looked different," I said.

It's funny how you spend five days a week at school with other kids, but only get to know a few of them properly. After chatting to Maisie for the past hour, I now knew more about her than I had learnt in a whole year at school. Amongst other things, I now knew that she also had an annoying younger sibling and she liked corny jokes... but only if they were good ones!

"I'm hungry," she said.

"I could see if I can find us some grubs to eat," I told her.

She looked alarmed. "You're not serious!"

"Of course I'm serious. Luke taught us about it at bush craft camp yesterday, remember?" I said. "If you find the right ones, they're packed full of nutrition. Worms, ants, beetles..."

"Go on then," she challenged. "You eat one."

"You're the one who's hungry, not me!" I retaliated, ignoring the grumble my stomach involuntarily let out, as if trying to prove me wrong. I wished that I hadn't gobbled down all my lunch when we first set off.

"Your noisy tummy says otherwise," Maisie said smugly. "Look, there's loads of ants on that tree stump. Think of all that nutrition," she teased. "Unless you're too chicken of course."

149

"Of course I'm not chicken," I said quickly. "I just don't fancy ants today. If it was a worm I'd do it." I quickly glanced around hoping there were no worms in sight.

"You are chicken," Maisie laughed. "Don't worry, I won't tell anyone. Remember, what happens in the forest, stays in the forest." She tried to move herself forward to change position as her leg was going a bit numb. She suddenly put her hand to her head and closed her eyes.

"Are you OK, Maisie?" I asked, feeling concerned.

"I just feel a bit dizzy," she said.

She looked a little pale which worried me.

"I think you need a drink of water," I said. "It's getting hot again now the storm has passed."

"I don't know where my bottle is," she replied with her eyes still closed. "I think it fell from my bag with my lunch when I slipped down here."

Without hesitation, I grabbed my own rucksack and pulled my bottle out of the side pocket. "Here, have mine," I said as I handed it to her.

Not even attempting to resist, she gladly accepted it and took four huge gulps.

"Thanks Ben," she said as she opened her eyes a crack. "I didn't realise how thirsty I was."

There were now only a few mouthfuls of water left in the bottle. I saved them for Maisie in case she needed a bit more later. I was sure the teachers would find us soon anyway. At least, I hoped they would. I didn't fancy being out here when it started to get dark.

CHAPTER 19

I glanced down at Maisie who was lying with her head on her rucksack and her foot resting on the ferns. After convincing her to remover her trainer and sock, I could see her ankle swelling before my eyes. I could almost see the flesh pulsating in and out where it was throbbing. We had been waiting for what felt like hours and Maisie had turned quite pale with the pain.

"How are you feeling?" I asked her.

"Not great," she replied.

Her change of tone concerned me. She was obviously really struggling if she couldn't even be bothered to be sarcastic anymore.

"Here, have a sip of this," I said, handing her my water bottle. My throat felt as dry as the time Pocket Rocket had tricked me into eating a 'sand pie' when we were young.

After Maisie had taken a sip, she

handed the near empty bottle back to me. I had the urge to take an enormous gulp to quench my thirst but forced myself to take just a tiny little drop instead. Just enough to wet my tongue to stop it from permanently fixing itself to the roof of my mouth.

"Surely they should be here by now," Maisie said in a voice that was etched with pain.

"They'll be here any minute now... I'm sure of it." I reassured her.

"Wanna bet?" she said.

"OK," I replied. "I bet you five packets of sweets from my secret school camp tuck shop that we'll be rescued in the next half an hour."

"OK, you're on," she said. "But what do I have to give you if I'm wrong?"

I thought for a second. "If I win the bet, you have to give me the bottle of Coke you have hidden under your bed!"

"How did you know about that?" exclaimed Maisie.

Tapping my nose, I gave her a smug look and told her that I wouldn't reveal my sources. In truth I had just overheard her telling Sophia about it when we were climbing onto the coach back at school, but she didn't need to know that. If it hadn't been so dry, my mouth would have watered at the thought of the fizzy, cold liquid pouring down my throat. I would never take drinking for granted again.

Moments later, we heard voices shouting in the distance. "BEN... MAISIE... BEN... MAISIE!"

Looking at each other with wide eyes, we shouted back in relief. "We're down here, HELP! Down here!"

"We've found them," shouted a familiar deep voice.

"How are you doing down there kids?"

"Fine thanks," I shouted back.

Maisie looked at me like I had suddenly grown two heads. "Fine?" she said "FINE? How is this fine?" she shrieked gesturing towards her ankle that was now nearing the size of an elephant's leg.

"OK, OK" I said, holding my hands up in apology. "Erm, NOT FINE," I shouted back.

"Better?" I asked, raising my eyebrows at Maisie.

"Are either of you hurt?" came back the

voice.

"Maisie's broken her ankle," I shouted back.

"I knew it!" she shrieked. "You thought it was broken all along didn't you!"

"No, of course not," I lied.

"Maybe just sprained," I shouted back unconvincingly.

"OK, I'm coming down," the voice shouted to us.

Next thing we knew, Luke, with a rope tied round his waist, expertly abseiled down the soggy steep hill. He was wearing chunky army-style boots which gripped the ground effortlessly.
The same ground we had slid down just hours before, as though we were on a waterslide.

"Alright kids," he said, as he reached the bottom. "I've come to get you back to your teachers."

We smiled gratefully at him. It wasn't like we were

stuck in the jungle hundreds of miles from civilisation. It was just the Isle of Wight. But still, part of me had been scared that we would be stuck there all night before help came.

"Ooh, that does look sore," he said as he looked at Maisie's ankle. I'm not sure we're going to get you up that slippery hill with you in that state. Ben, you can climb up with me by using the rope. Maisie, we're going to need to get you out by helicopter!"

As Luke reached for his walkie-talkie to contact the rest of his rescue team, Maisie and I caught each other's eyes and erupted into uncontrollable laughter. This time it was Maisie who started deliriously singing the *Fireman Sam* tune.

CHAPTER 20

After hefty negotiations, aka, me begging a
lot, Luke had allowed us both to be rescued
by helicopter.

Maisie had helped by telling Luke how she
would be absolutely terrified without me
there and she would refuse to go if I
couldn't come too. I made a mental note to
repay her by not taking the bottle of Coke
she had under her bed which was now
rightfully mine by winning the bet. We had

literally flown straight to the hospital which was only minutes away given how small the Isle of Wight actually is, and landed right on the roof. The journey became far less exciting from then on, as Maisie was rushed to the accident and emergency ward to get her ankle seen to, and I was met by Mr Wallis who took me back to Camp Komodo in a taxi under full interrogation as to how it had happened.

It was much later that Maisie also returned to the camp with her ankle in a plaster cast.

"Just a sprain, hey Ben," she said as I snuck out of my safari tent to see how she was when I heard the rumour that she was back.

I smiled at her sheepishly. "I knew it was broken," I admitted. "I just didn't want to worry you."

"I know," she said. "Thanks for looking after me, Ben."

"That's OK," I said as I handed her a packet of softmints.

"What's this for?" she asked.

"Just a little something from the secret school camp tuck shop to say sorry for making you keep going in the storm when you wanted to take shelter."

"It's honestly not your fault, Ben," she said. "It was an adventure. My ankle will be fine in six weeks and we'll be laughing about it all before we know it. Just remember, what happened in the forest stays in the forest," she said looking at me intently with a hidden message in her eyes. I knew that she meant I mustn't tell anyone about her pee'ing her pants as she fell down the hill. She needn't have worried though. If there was one thing I was good at, it was keeping a secret.

CHAPTER 21

It was Thursday night, our last night at
Camp Komodo. Maisie's parents had come
to collect her that morning despite her
pleas to stay until the end of camp. I felt
really bad for her but knew there wasn't an
awful lot she could do with a broken ankle.

Our final day whizzed by as we got to try
out loads of water sports in the sea. We
tried kayaking and sailing, and even got to
do some body boarding in the waves.
Tommy was hilarious and had us all falling
about with laughter as he attempted to
stand up on the body board and face
planted straight into the water.

We were having such an amazing time that none of us wanted to go home. But, all too quickly, our last evening had arrived, and after our final yummy dinner where I filled my stomach with not just seconds but thirds as well, the teachers announced that we were going to have an awards ceremony. We were all told to go back to our rooms and put our smartest clothes on. We had to return to the main dining room at 7pm.

Rushing back to our safari tent, Tommy, Jayden, Charlie, Noah, Ryan and I, all flopped down on our beds. I had definitely lucked out with my room mates. After initially staying up late on our first night, we were so exhausted after the day's activities that we had usually crashed out by 10.30pm. We took it in turns throughout the night to throw pillows at Ryan when he snored too loudly and woke us up, but apart from that we had all gotten on pretty well.

There was a knock at the door.

"What's the password?" shouted Noah and Charlie in unison.

"Erm, Boys Rule?" came Mr Skills' voice from the other side of the door.

We all looked at each other with raised eyebrows wondering why a teacher was knocking and guessing a password rather than just bolshily coming in like you'd expect.

"Nope, wrong answer," Jayden shouted back.

"How about Girls Stink?" Mr Skills tried again.

We all laughed in surprise. "Nope, wrong again," I shouted this time.

"Come on boys, just let me in," pleaded Mr Skills.

"You know you can just pull the zip up and let yourself in, Mr Skills," shouted Tommy.

The zip moved upwards and the safari tent door opened wide to reveal Mr Skills standing there looking slightly flustered.

"Are you OK Mr Skills?" I asked.

"I need a favour," he replied.

This was weird. Since when did teachers ask kids for favours?

"I need to buy something from your secret school camp tuck shop."

I coughed to hide my surprise at what he'd said. I had not been expecting that.

"But, I don't have a secret school camp tuck shop," I lied as I crossed my fingers behind my back.

"Come on, Ben, of course you do! I heard the girls whispering about it yesterday."

I looked around at my roommates suspiciously. Was this a trick? Had Mrs Jackson guessed that I had been running a secret tuck shop whilst we had been away and asked Mr Skills to try and catch me out? I wasn't taking any chances.

"Sorry Mr Skills, but I think you must have misheard. Maybe what you actually heard the girls saying was they liked my secret 'duck top'. And," I added, "it's a secret because I'm a bit embarrassed about it."

Mr Skills looked at me, weighing up whether or not I was telling the truth.

"You see Mr Skills, I had a toy duck once called Professor Duck and I was really sad when I gave him away so my mum bought me a top to remind me of him... a top with a picture of a duck on it."

I made my eyes go wide and innocent like Pocket Rocket did when he wanted something from Mum.

"It's true," said Tommy, backing me up from his bunk bed underneath mine. "But, please don't tell anyone as Ben is very sensitive about it."

I heard a muffled noise from the other side of the room as Noah hid his face in his pillow so that Mr Skills couldn't hear him laughing.

"OK, well if you say so," said Mr Skills, not looking convinced. "I'll leave you boys to get ready, but if any of you do happen to find that you have something along the lines of a Mars Bar or a Snickers or anything chocolatey really, then I'd be willing to pay £1 for it."

My business brain kicked in. Money was money after all, and Mr Skills did genuinely seem to just be having a big chocolate craving.

"Would a packet of strawberry laces do Mr Skills?" I asked. "Not from a secret tuck shop of course. I just happen to have one here in my bag that my mum gave me."

Mr Skills' eyes lit up. "Well, it's not quite the chocolate I was after but it's better than nothing," he said, holding a £1 coin out to me.

Knowing a sugar craving when I saw one, I shook my head slowly at him. "Sorry Mr Skills, but this is the only one I have and I'm afraid I can't let it go for less than £2."

CHAPTER 22

Smugly patting my pocket where two £1 coins now sat nestled in, thanks to Mr Skills, I took a seat on a chair next to Tommy in anticipation of the awards ceremony.

Being told to dress smartly meant that I was now wearing a pair of shorts with no mud on them and a T-shirt with just a tiny bit of ketchup down it. Well what did the teachers expect? It was the last day of a school camp. As if I would have any clean clothes left!

"OK, kids," shouted Mrs Jackson above the noise of all sixty of us talking at once. "It's time for this year's Camp Komodo awards!"

We all started clapping and cheering as we got into the spirit of it.

"First off," shouted Mrs Jackson, "we have the award for the tidiest camper."

Urgh, I rolled my eyes at Tommy. That had to be the most boring award ever. I seriously hoped they could do better than that otherwise the next hour was going to be very boring.

"Which goes to Sebastian!" she announced.

Sebastian from the other class stepped forward to accept his award. Or more  specifically, a certificate with his name on it and "Tidiest Camper" written in bold bubbly letters at the top. He beamed from ear to ear, like he had won an Oscar.

"Well done Sebastian," said Mrs Jackson. "Never have I seen such a perfectly arranged clothes drawer in all my years of coming to camp."

Tommy and I looked at each other and giggled. The only thing our drawer was used for was hiding the secret school camp tuck shop goodies when the teachers sprung a room inspection on us!

An array of awards followed including 'early bird camper' which went to Katie who woke up raring to go at 5am every morning

much to the distress of her fellow roommates, and 'bravest camper' which unsurprisingly went to Sophia for the fearless way in which she tackled the activities such as the swing of trust.

"And the next award of the night," continued Mrs Jackson, "goes to 'Most Surprising Camper'. Now, the thing I love about doing these camps is that as teachers, we get to know all of you on a different level. We see a side to you that we don't see at school. And I absolutely love it when I see a shy child come out of themselves and their true personality shines through. This year, the award is going to someone who has shown himself to be not just the kind, thoughtful boy that we all know but also one with an amazing sense of humour and someone with an awful lot to say for himself when you have the time to chat to him. This year, I am delighted to say that this award goes to Tommy!"

I cheered when I heard my best friend's name and gave him a pat on the back. I was so pleased that everyone was getting to know the Tommy that I knew. I watched him walk up to receive his certificate and thought, not for the first time, how lucky I was to have a best friend like him. Blushing from cheek to cheek, Tommy returned to his seat next to me to hear the rest of the awards.

I wasn't expecting to get one. After all, I wasn't the tidiest, or the most helpful, or the cutest. I may have stood a chance of the best at orienteering, but given that I had ended up falling down a steep muddy hill and being rescued by a helicopter, I had pretty much done myself out of that prize. I thought I might have possibly got one of the token funny awards such as smelliest socks, or messiest hair, but no such luck there either. It made my day when the bossiest camper award went to Evil Emily. She did not look one bit pleased when she went up to accept that one!

Then, just as the awards were coming to a close, Mrs Jackson announced one last final award – the award for the 'most loyal camper.'

"Now this," Mrs Jackson announced, "is always a favourite award of mine to give. And this year the teachers and the camp helpers were unanimous on who it should go to. This award, this year, goes to a person who put someone else's needs before his own. Someone who took care of another person when they needed it. Someone who went thirsty so that someone else could drink. Someone who made someone else feel safe even though they must have been scared themselves. Boys and girls, this year, the award for the most loyal camper goes to none other than Ben Collins!"

I stood up to the applause of all my classmates, not quite believing it.

I had thought that the teachers would be mad at me for making the wrong decision to keep walking in the storm. Instead, they were congratulating me for how I had looked after Maisie afterwards.

"Your competitive streak won over in pushing your team on through that storm when you should have taken shelter, Ben. We all make mistakes, but it's how we learn from those mistakes that matters. It's how we act in the future that matters. And how you looked after Maisie when she was hurt and waited for help demonstrated a loyal friend that every one of us would be lucky to have in our lives. So, Ben Collins, I give this last award of the night to you, Most Loyal Camper!"

CHAPTER 23

As I walked through my front door I was immediately bundled by Big Spud, Little Spud, Obi and Lola. As Obi and Lola wagged their tails and licked my face, my two youngest brothers simultaneously sat on me demanding to know what presents I had brought them back.

"Get off me and I'll show you," I laughed as Obi's tongue poked my left nostril. Hearing the word 'presents', Pocket Rocket also miraculously appeared in the hallway.

"Where's my present?" he demanded.

"Erm, aren't you lot going to say hello to

your brother first?" Mum said as she expertly plucked Big Spud and Little Spud from me.

"Did you miss me?" I asked them.

"Nope," said Pocket Rocket, "not one bit."

"What about you two?" I asked, pointing at my other brothers.

Two little voices said "Nope" in unison whilst shaking their heads.

"You porky pie-ers!" exclaimed Mum. "You know full well you missed your brother!"

"No we didn't," said Big Spud.

"Then why did you and Little Spud sleep top to tail in Ben's bed every night that he was away?" asked Mum smugly.

"And, why did you shout out Ben's name in your sleep last night, Pocket Rocket?" she said, raising her eyebrows at him.

"I was probably dreaming that he was annoying me," said Pocket Rocket sulkily.

"Ah OK, so I must have misheard you when you shouted out 'Ben, let's make Little Spud eat a slug and tell Mum Big Spud made him do it.'"

Pocket Rocket started laughing. "Oh yeah, I did dream that last night! That was a good dream!"

"Hmm," said Mum with her 'mum-look-of-disapproval' face on.

"So, can we have our presents now Ben," asked Little Spud, trying to look angelic.

"Only if you say please," I said, enjoying the power I had over my little brothers right then. "And, why were you in my bed? I told you all to stay out of my room or I'd let the stink bombs off."

Big Spud and Little Spud giggled. "We went in on purpose to see if they would go off," said Little Spud.

"Turns out you were lying," Big Spud added smugly.

"Now, pleeeeeease can we have our presents," they all drawled in unison.

I grabbed my rucksack and fished around for the presents that I had bought them on the ferry on the way home. For Pocket Rocket, there was a giant tube of very sickly looking sweets which he looked delighted about.

"Thanks Ben," he said before running back to the lounge to continue his game of Fifa on the Xbox.

I'd got Big Spud and Little Spud matching teddy bears wearing T-shirts saying 'I Love the Isle Of Wight' on them.

Their little hands greedily grabbed them before they ran off together, shouting something about taking them down the slide.

There was one more tiny teddy bear left in my bag for my little sister, Jodie. I'd give that to her when I next went to see my other dad, Rob. I had wondered if I could get away with not getting her something and treat myself to a giant tube of sweets like I had bought for Pocket Rocket, but then I felt guilty. She may not live with us, but she was still my baby sister.

"So, how about you tell me all about your amazing week over a lovely mug of hot chocolate and marshmallows?" Mum asked me as she hugged me into her.

I yawned as I followed her into the kitchen. I was exhausted.

"There's not really much to tell," I said. "I stayed in this really cool safari tent, the food was way better than your cooking, and Tommy face planted the sea when we went body boarding."

"Sounds fun," Mum said, overlooking my comment about her cooking. "What else did you do?"

"Not much," I replied lazily. "Just a bit of kayaking, and sailing... and we went on this huge swing thing over a cliff where you would have totally splatted if you fell out, and you had to trust the other kids to stop you swinging... oh, and we got trapped in the woods in a huge thunderstorm... and a tree nearly hit me and Maisie... and we fell down this steep slope, and she broke her ankle... and we had to be rescued by helicopter."

I took a sip of my hot chocolate through the sticky marshmallows and looked up at Mum. She was staring at me wide-eyed, looking shocked, and then broke into a smile.

"Haha, good one Ben, I nearly believed you then. I'm so gullible. I can't believe I nearly fell for that. So what did you really do all week then?"

I was about to insist that I hadn't made it all up when Big Spud came charging into the kitchen.

"Mum, Mum, Little Spud has got his head stuck in a flower pot. He said his teddy told him to do it!"

This I had to see. Following Mum and Big Spud out the back door I thought to myself how good it was to be home!

OTHER BOOKS IN THE SERIES

ABOUT THE AUTHOR

Kerry Gibb is a mum to four boys. Their never ending antics and awesome sense of humour gave her all the inspiration she needed to write the It's A Kid's Life series.

Kerry graduated from The University Of Sussex in 1999 with a degree in Social Psychology, where she took a particular interest in the development of children. She now regularly visits schools to promote reading and writing to children and to inspire all the budding authors out there.

Kerry's favourite saying is 'Reach for the moon and even if you miss you will be among the stars.'
Follow Kerry on Instagram, Facebook, Twitter and YouTube!
If you loved reading this book as much as Kerry loved writing it, make sure you leave a review on Amazon and www.kerrygibb.com

ACKNOWLEDGEMENTS

As always, thank you first and foremost to all my readers – children and parents alike. Seeing your enthusiasm for the It's A Kid's Life series is what spurs me on to write more. The encouragement from you all whilst I have been writing this fifth book has been amazing! May all your school residentials be as exciting as Ben's!

Thank you to my favourite four people in the whole world, my sons – Liam, Jamie, Danny and Joe. It is lovely watching them grow up with these books. Without the constant chaos they cause, my life would be very dull!

Thank you to my amazingly talented illustrator, Helen Poole, for being able to put the pictures that I create in my mind into a reality.

Thank you to my editor, Michelle Misra, for bringing my book to the next level with her invaluable expertise.

I must, as always, thank my cocker spaniels, Obi and Lola, for always being by my side as I write. Their fur therapy is truly amazing.

I have loved every second of writing this book, and hope you all love reading it just as much.